"We Both Want To Get You To San Philippe As Soon As Possible. And Without Any Scandal. Don't We?"

"Yes, of course." Lexie swallowed. "Can I point out that your being in my room at three in the morning is probably not the best way to go about that?"

"Probably not."

She waited for him to move. And waited. "If you're finished, I guess you can go."

He stepped behind her. As she shrugged the jacket from her shoulders he slipped his hands beneath her hair to grasp the collar, his knuckles skimming her neck. Her eyes met his in the mirror as he drew the garment down her arms. For a second their gazes locked. It was as though he were undressing her and she was allowing it. Sudden heat suffused her, coalescing deep inside her.

Lexie closed her eyes so he wouldn't be able to read her response—part confusion and part...desire.

Dear Reader,

One of the pleasures of having children is that they give you a legitimate excuse to watch children's movies. And one of my favorites is the story of Shrek, the ogre who has to rescue Princess Fiona and deliver her to Lord Farquaad, never dreaming that he'll fall in love with her along the way.

His Bride for the Taking is my twist on the Shrek story. Rafe, a man enjoying his bachelor existence, has one simple job to do—escort Lexie back to his country so that she can begin a courtship with his brother. How difficult can it be? Deliciously difficult, as it turns out.

I hope you enjoy reading Rafe and Lexie's story.

Warmest wishes,

Sandra Hyatt

SANDRA HYATT

HIS BRIDE FOR THE TAKING

Published by Silhouette Books

America's Publisher of Contemporary Romance

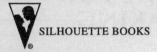

SILHOUETTE BOOKS

ISBN-13: 978-0-373-73035-3

HIS BRIDE FOR THE TAKING

Recycling programs
for this product may
not exist in your area.

This edition published by arrangement with Harlequin Books S.A.

For questions and comments about the quality of this book please contact us at Customer_eCare@Harlequin.ca.

® and TM are trademarks of Harlequin Books S.A., used under license. Trademarks indicated with ® are registered in the United States Patent and Trademark Office, the Canadian Trade Marks Office and in other countries.

Visit Silhouette Books at www.eHarlequin.com

Printed in U.S.A.

Books by Sandra Hyatt

Silhouette Desire

Having the Billionaire's Baby #1956
The Magnate's Pregnancy Proposal #1991
His Bride for the Taking #2022

SANDRA HYATT

After completing a business degree, traveling and then settling into a career in marketing, *USA TODAY* bestselling author Sandra Hyatt was relieved to experience one of life's eureka! moments while on maternity leave—she discovered that writing books, although a lot slower, was just as much fun as reading them.

She knows life doesn't always hand out happy endings and figures that's why books ought to. She loves being along for the journey with her characters as they work around, over and through the obstacles standing in their way.

Sandra has lived in both the U.S. and England and currently lives near the coast in New Zealand with her high school sweetheart and their two children.

You can visit her at www.sandrahyatt.com.

To Abby Gaines, Karina Bliss and Tessa Radley.
Fabulous writers and wonderful women.
Your friendship and support, wisdom and laughter
are treasures of this journey.

One

Glancing at her watch, Lexie Wyndham Jones hurried from the stables and through a back entrance of her family's Massachusetts home. The ride had taken longer than she'd intended, but she still had time to prepare herself.

Dropping onto the seat just inside the door, she began wrestling one of her riding boots off. At the sound of someone clearing his throat, she looked up to see their butler standing close, watching her. "May I be of assistance, miss?"

He had his stoic expression on, all droopy gray eyebrows and even droopier jowls. "No. I'm fine. Thank you, Stanley." He always offered. She always refused. It had been their routine since Lexie had first learned to ride. The boot came free in her hands and she dropped it to the floor.

When Stanley altered the routine by not then moving away, she glanced up.

"Your mother has been looking for you."

Sighing, Lexie turned her attention to her unyielding second boot. "What have I done now?"

"Your…prince has come."

For a second, Lexie froze. And Stanley, against every fiber of his butler being, allowed his disapproval to show. He hadn't said, he never would, but he thought she and her mother were making a mistake. She redoubled her efforts on her boot, hiding her surge of elation. The boot came free in her hands and she dropped it beside the first and stood. "He's early." Perhaps he had been so eager to see her that—

"I believe with the changeover of your mother's secretary there has been some confusion about the times. The prince was of the impression that you would be accompanying him back to San Philippe this afternoon."

"But the dinner?"

"Precisely."

"Mother has explained?"

"Of course. You'll be leaving in the morning as planned."

"Oh, dear." She didn't suppose it was good practice to thwart a prince's expectations, but it couldn't be any worse than thwarting her mother's.

"Precisely." The merest twinkle glinted in Stanley's gray eyes, and she got the feeling there was something he wasn't telling her. No doubt she'd find out soon enough.

"Where are they now?"

"The croquet lawn."

"I'd better get out there." She turned, but stopped at the sound of Stanley again clearing his throat.

"Perhaps you would like to freshen up first?"

Lexie scanned her mud-splattered jodhpurs and laughed. "Holy—" She stopped herself in time and winked. "Good heavens, yes." She mimicked her mother's cultured tones. "Thank you, Stanley."

He inclined his head.

Thirty minutes later, Lexie, now wearing a demure—and clean—sundress, lowered herself into the chair in the arbor. A dark jacket lay draped over the arm of the chair next to her. Drawn to touch it, Lexie trailed her fingers over the sun-warmed leather and the exquisitely soft silk of the lining.

Pulling her hand to her lap, she took in the croquet game that looked close to ending. There were only two people on the lawn: broad-shouldered Adam, his back to her, lining up a shot, and her fiercely slender mother. It was easy to tell from the rigid set to her mother's shoulders and the too-bright society laugh that drifted across the lawn that Antonia was losing. A result that didn't bode well. Her mother didn't quite have the power of the Queen of Hearts—no one would lose their head. Not literally. But…

Lexie watched with surprise as Adam swung his mallet and played a merciless shot, sending her mother's ball careering miles from where she'd want it. While she wouldn't expect him to throw a game, she would have thought he'd be more tactful. He was renowned as a master diplomat, and he usually managed to charm her mother. The tinkling laughter that followed his shot was anything but charmed, and Lexie cringed.

Adam straightened and turned, and her heart beat a little faster in anticipation. Then she caught his profile, and her breath stalled in her chest as she looked and, disbelieving, looked again.

Not Adam Marconi, crown prince of San Philippe.

But his brother, Rafe.

A heated flush swept up her face.

As if sensing her scrutiny, Rafe turned fully. Across half the lawn his gaze caught hers. Slowly, he inclined his head, almost as Stanley did, but with Stanley the gesture, though it could convey a dozen nuanced meanings, was usually genial or at least respectful. Rafe's nod, the stiff little bow, even from this distance, communicated displeasure.

Which made two of them. She did *not* want to see Rafe.

Fighting for composure, Lexie had to remind herself, as her mother so often did, that she, too, had royal bloodlines, her ancestors having once ruled the small European principality that Rafe's father was sovereign of. A Wyndham Jones was cool and self-possessed at all times. Supposedly.

Lexie wasn't a particularly good example of the name, but she tried. As the shock of seeing Rafe ebbed, it was replaced by disappointment and chagrin. Adam, her prince, hadn't come himself, but rather his profligate brother. The Playboy Prince, as the press called him. Or, as Lexie secretly thought of him, the Frog Prince. Nothing to do with his looks—he was Adonis personified. Even on the croquet lawn his fluid athleticism was obvious. Michelangelo's David come to life. The confidence that came from the unique combination of his position in the world and his looks pervaded everything about him.

Her mother, following Rafe's gaze, saw Lexie and abandoned the game to glide across the lawn, probably convincing herself she'd been about to win. Rafe strolled in her wake. And though he appeared relaxed, she couldn't help but feel he was zeroing in on her like an Armani-clad, heat-seeking missile. She watched him through narrowed eyes. Her mother crossed into her line of vision and scanned Lexie critically from head to toe, her expression a dire warning to behave herself.

Lexie's jaw clenched tighter, but as they neared her she forced her lips into a smile and extended her hand. Rafe reached for it, closed strong fingers around hers and then lifted her knuckles to his lips and pressed the gentlest of kisses there.

For as long as his touch lasted, confusion reigned. And in her surprise, Lexie forgot her anger, forgot her plans for her future, forgot her mother, even. She was aware only of being simultaneously swamped and stilled by sensation, warm lips and gentle fingers and the strange shiver of heat that coursed through her. Rafe lifted his head and she felt at close range the burning connection of his gaze from dark, honey-colored eyes.

As he released her fingers, her presence of mind

returned and she remembered everything, recognized his tactic as some kind of power play. "It's a pleasure to meet you again, Your Highness," she said through her most practiced smile.

He returned a smile that hid the irritation she'd glimpsed earlier. "Rafe will do. Unless you'd also prefer me to call you Miss Wyndham Jones."

"No." Lexie shook her head.

"In that case, Alexia, the pleasure is all mine. It's been too long."

She bit down on the word *liar* that wanted to escape her lips, partly because it would be so terribly impolite, but mainly because she, too, had lied. Nothing about this meeting was the pleasure it should have been. "And such a surprise, too. I must confess, I was expecting Adam." Thoughtful, gentlemanly, mature Adam.

One corner of Rafe's lips lifted in a mocking smile. "You usually are, as I recall."

Lexie felt her face pale. How dare he? One mistake. Four years ago. A mistake she'd fervently hoped he'd forgotten. After all, to a man like him it was an event that could barely have registered. It should have been nothing to him. It *was* nothing, she reminded herself. An accident, a misunderstanding.

At a glittering masquerade ball, if you had just turned eighteen, it was easy to confuse one masked prince's identity with another's, particularly when their hair and builds were so similar. And if that prince waltzed you to a quiet corner behind a fluted marble column and kissed you, gently at first and then as though you were ambrosia itself, coaxing an unguarded response in return, then when he unmasked you and realized who you were, staggered backward, cursing under his breath...

"I'm afraid I must apologize on my brother's behalf." Rafe's tone, though still formal, had softened, and he sounded almost sincere. Of course, he, too, would regret that it wasn't Adam here instead of him. "Royal duties prevented him coming to escort you back to San Philippe. He is, however, greatly looking forward to your arrival."

It took an effort of will not to roll her eyes. Greatly looking forward to? Could he be any more formal? And still the word *liar* simmered in her consciousness. Because despite the fact that she'd had a crush on Adam for almost as long as she could remember, and that she knew Adam *liked* her, and that for years the possibility of a match between them had been promoted by their respective parents, their correspondence was hardly much more than friendly.

But things were about to change. Adam hadn't seen her in four years. He was about to meet the new, improved, grown-up Alexia Wyndham Jones.

"In the meantime, unfortunately," Rafe said, "you'll have to make do with me."

"Oh, not unfortunate at all," her mother interjected before Lexie could respond. Under Rafe's questioning gaze, Lexie swallowed her retort. Probably for the best. This man, as well as potentially being her brother-in-law, was apparently her pathway to her future, and she would do what needed to be done to ensure nothing went wrong now. Not when she was this close to setting her life on its proper course.

Rafe was no more than a temporary inconvenience.

"Alexia was reminiscing just yesterday about her last visit to San Philippe," said her mother. "I don't believe you were there at the time."

"I was gone for most of it, but I did arrive back in time for her final evening and the masquerade ball." A hint of amusement and challenge laced his voice.

One stupid, mistaken kiss. Why did he have to be so intent on reminding her of it?

"The ball. I'd almost forgotten about that." Lexie smiled sweetly. "It was so overshadowed by everything else I saw and did while I was there."

Rafe's lips stretched into a grin, and a roguish gleam lit those dark eyes. "I shall have to see if I can remind you, seeing as it's all we shared of that visit. I recall your gown in particular, a deep burgundy, and it had—"

Lexie laughed, sounding scarily like her mother, but at least cutting short anything further Rafe might have said. The gown had featured a daringly low back. When they'd danced, his fingertips had caressed her skin, trailing sparks of heat. "I can scarcely remember what I wore yesterday, let alone four years ago. As for reminding me of that last visit, there's no need. I'm sure I'll make enough new memories in the future." She looked pointedly at him.

Her words, or her glance, seemed to recall Rafe to his purpose here. Not to discomfit her by reminding her of a kiss that was best forgotten because it should never have happened, but to escort her to his country so she could get to know his brother better and more important, for Adam to get to know her better. *Courtship* was the word her mother had used—but only once, because apparently Lexie had found it "inappropriately amusing."

Rafe straightened and took a step back. The gleam in his eyes disappeared, his expression hardening into regal arrogance.

"Dinner will be served at eight," her mother said, oblivious to the tension and displeasure arcing between them. "I've invited a few close friends, and some of your countrymen."

It promised to be a tedious, stuffy affair. Lexie could almost have pitied him if she hadn't been so annoyed and if he weren't so far above needing that sentiment from her. He was the one who would be on display tonight, not only for his countrymen but for friends of her mother's eager to be able to boast of their dinner with European royalty. Lexie, on the other hand, would be able to slip away relatively early.

"I look forward to it," Rafe said, sounding as though he meant it.

Liar.

Rafe tossed his dinner jacket over the back of the armchair in his room. He'd attended more boring dinners in his life than he could possibly count, but tonight's ranked among the worst. If it hadn't been for the presence of Tony, an old school friend, now a high-powered Boston attorney, the evening would have been unbearable.

Out of curiosity, he'd closely watched the woman who

hoped to snare herself a prince—his brother's would-be bride—throughout the evening. She had shown scarcely any reaction as her mother, none too subtly, toasted her success in her forthcoming travels. His observation of her served only to confirm that she was a perfect match for Adam. Demure, respectable, quiet and a gracious hostess. In a word, boring.

Even the dress she'd worn, a silvery high-necked thing that she'd teamed with pearls, had been boring. She had a passable figure, curves where they should be, yet she did nothing to accentuate her assets. She wore her glossy auburn hair swept back from her face into a sleek—boring—knot. He had seen no trace of the spark he'd imagined in her moss-green eyes this afternoon as she'd tried to challenge him.

She'd clearly been irritated that it was he who'd come for her. Tough luck. If she wanted to be Adam's wife, she'd have to learn to hide that flash of her eyes that revealed those emotions. And if she wanted to marry into his family, she'd do well to learn that more often than not royal considerations overrode personal ones. His presence here was a case in point. If it had been up to him, he would have spent the day playing polo and the evening dancing with the charming divorcée he'd met at a charity gala last week.

But Rafe's father, Prince Henri Augustus Marconi, claiming failing health and impatient to secure the family line, had, in a fit of regal autocracy, decreed that it was Adam's duty to marry—and marry well and soon—and that the heiress Alexia Wyndham Jones was the perfect candidate.

Rafe had at first thought the announcement a joke. His sister, Rebecca, had been shocked at their father's methods, though not his choice. She liked Alexia. Adam, being Adam, had let nothing of his thoughts show, except to say he wasn't able to get away from San Philippe. And somehow Rafe, still atoning for his latest scandal, and possibly his burst of laughter, had ended up here playing babysitter and escort.

Not long after the dinner was finished Alexia had claimed a headache and excused herself, leaving him without even the distraction of watching her as he made conversation with one after another of her mother's guests. He'd almost wished he could use the same excuse as she had just to get away from the endless pretension.

At the throaty rumble of an engine, he looked out his window to see a Harley Davidson carrying two leather-clad riders disappear into the night.

He removed his cufflinks, dropping them onto the antique dresser, and flicked a glance at his watch. The other good thing about catching up with Tony was that his friend had been able to fill him in on the best Boston night spots. If he couldn't be in his own country, he could as least make the most of being here.

Ten minutes later he slid behind the wheel of the car that had been arranged for him and pulled out of the garage and onto the Wyndham Joneses' driveway.

And a mere thirty minutes later, Rafe stood by Tony on the mezzanine level of the recommended club, watching the throng on the dance floor below him and wondering if coming here hadn't been a mistake. He could have been in any one of a dozen exclusive nightclubs around the world. Here, conversation was near impossible. One a.m. and the place heaved with dancers and the beat of the music. Artificial smoke swirled about the dance floor, colored lights cast eerie illumination on the faces, bodies and limbs of the dancers.

There was only one thing—one person—who piqued his curiosity. His attention kept returning to her, and he couldn't figure out why. She was familiar and yet not. Black hair, cut into a precise bob, swayed around her face as she moved to the music. The haircut and her darkly made-up eyes brought to mind Cleopatra. She danced opposite a tall, brawny man, dark hair, dark skin, possibly South American, who moved almost as well as she did. And yet, with her eyes often closed and her partner continuously scanning the crowd, she looked more as if she were dancing alone.

There was something entrancing, an innate sensuality, about the way she seemed aware of only the music and her own body—a svelte body sheathed in a subtly shimmering black dress that was almost nunlike compared to some of the outfits here tonight. But though it revealed little skin other than that of her graceful arms and a generous but still disappointing portion of her long legs, it molded lovingly to her curves and her slender waist.

Rafe wasn't the only one who noticed. From his elevated position he could see that she drew more than her share of admiring—drooling—glances.

"Who's that?" He almost had to shout in Tony's ear to be heard.

Tony followed his gaze. "The blonde? An actress, I think. Or maybe a singer? Wasn't she on the cover of the tabloids last week? The press are always after her."

Rafe saw the woman Tony meant, a Barbie doll clone. "No. Cleopatra. Over to the right a little."

Tony frowned. "Don't know. I've seen her here a couple of times. Asked her to dance once. She turned me down flat, then turned her back on me. Seems to prefer them six foot four and burly."

Rafe watched as a man with the loudest red shirt he had ever seen tried to cut in with Cleopatra. Tall and Brawny looked at his partner and she gave her head the faintest shake. He said something to Red Shirt, who scowled and then turned back to his cluster of laughing, and clearly inebriated, friends.

Rafe kept his gaze on the woman. There was something tantalizingly familiar about her. He had a good memory for faces and yet he couldn't place her.

"It happened just like that for me, too," Tony said dolefully.

Rafe laughed. "It's all in the execution."

"You think she'll dance with you? You're good, buddy, but you're not that good. She's different. Not interested."

Rafe seldom turned down a challenge, and after the boredom of the evening and the potential boredom of tomorrow, a day spent babysitting "Precious," he relished the fillip of Tony's unspoken dare even more. "Watch and learn, my friend. Watch and learn."

On the dance floor, he scarcely noticed the patrons parting to let him through. He fixed his gaze on

Cleopatra as he approached her from the side. Slender, toned arms were raised above her head. Her eyes were closed. Dark, curling lashes kissed her cheeks. A small, secretive smile played about her cherry-colored lips. She managed to look both vulnerable and untouchable.

Naturally making him want to touch.

Intrigued and appreciative, he felt an undeniable pull of attraction. She *would* dance with him, she had to. He wanted to learn how she would move when they danced together, he wanted to know the color of her eyes, he wanted to know the fullness of that smile. He wanted—

Like a bucket of cold water over his wants, recognition slammed through him.

Alexia.

Followed by denial. It couldn't be. Demure, boring Alexia was at home in bed with a headache.

He moved closer. She turned away, obscuring his view. But it was her. He knew it with absolute certainty. The porcelain skin, the almost stubborn jaw, and that something else, something hidden that he couldn't define.

He now also knew Tall and Brawny's role. Bodyguard. What he didn't know was what the hell she was doing here and, more important, what he should do about it. Did he leave her or get her out of here? She wasn't his responsibility. Yet. And chances were she'd get through the evening without a scandal.

Another of Red Shirt's group staggered her way.

Rafe flicked a glance at her partner, saw recognition of him dawn in Tall and Brawny's eyes. He signaled with a tilt of his head for the bodyguard to take care of Alexia's next would-be dance partner. The larger man nodded and stepped aside.

Two

Trying not to clench his jaw, Rafe watched Alexia dance. This woman who moved so sinuously and sensuously, lost in the music, was not the same bland woman who'd sat demurely through dinner.

She was playing some kind of game with them all.

He had no time for women who played games, women who pretended to be one thing when they were something else altogether. He was still dealing with the fallout from his last encounter with such a woman.

He was standing, arms folded, when Alexia finally opened her eyes. Her gaze alighted first on his chest, then snapped to his face. He caught the flash of horror, watched the horror schooled into a bright, false smile. "Sorry, I don't dance with other men." As if she might still get away with it. Without waiting for his response, she turned and slipped into the swirling crowd.

She didn't get far. He caught up with her at the edge of the dance floor as she tried to get past a cluster of tipsy women, one of them wearing a bridal veil, all of them shrieking with laughter.

He stilled Alexia with a hand on her slender, heated shoulder.

She spun around. "Go away," she said with a force that surprised him.

He'd lowered his hand as she turned, sliding it down the skin of her arm so that it now cupped her elbow. He leaned closer so she'd hear him over the music. "No." She stiffened at his refusal. "You're asking for trouble being in this place. My responsibility is to get you safely back to my country. The demure Alexia Wyndham Jones whom the people will love. Possibly their future princess. Someone they can look up to, bearing in mind that they're more conservative than you Americans. Not someone who dresses like, like…"

He faltered under the indignant heat of her gaze.

"Like what?" Her hands went to her hips, shaking off his touch. A mutinous expression tightened her lips. In truth there was nothing anyone could object to in what she was wearing. Anyone, apparently, except him. He couldn't put his finger on just what it was that bothered him. But it did bother him, and that was good enough for him. "Surely you don't need me to spell it out for you?" Damn, he sounded like his father. Master of the guilt trip.

Sudden resignation sagged through her body, and

he almost felt bad for it. After all, he'd been known on more than one occasion to skip out on official duties to have a little fun. And he knew what it was like to get busted.

But that was different.

Alexia was only twenty-two, and as well as being an heiress to millions, she might one day sit on the throne beside his brother. From what he knew of her, she'd led a cloistered existence. There was no end of trouble she could get into here. Very public trouble. The world was too full of predators, the press too greedy for gossip. Part of the reason her candidacy as a partner for Adam had been approved was her perceived innocence. Rafe glanced at the bodyguard hovering near her side. "Alexia and I need to have a little chat. A private chat."

The bodyguard looked at Alexia, she lifted her shoulders in a shrug. "It's okay, Mario. I may as well get this over with."

As the bodyguard moved a little farther off, Rafe leaned closer. "What exactly are you doing here?"

"Pardon?"

She'd heard him; she was just looking to delay answering, subtly challenging his right to even ask.

He leaned closer still—another millimeter and his body would be pressed against hers. Those lush, cherry-colored lips were clamped together. He caught her scent, something with an underlying zing of fresh citrus, and he felt the heat of her body radiating from her. Pushing a lock of the ridiculous dark hair—nowhere near as attractive as her natural auburn—behind her delicate ear, he put his lips close. "We'll talk in my car."

She tensed. "We don't need to talk."

Another patron passed too close, knocking into Rafe, who knocked into Alexia. His grip tightened around her.

Suddenly, flashes went off, blinding in their brightness. Rafe pulled Alexia hard against his chest, shielding her face and turning so his back was to the continuing pop of the flashes.

Damn. The paparazzi were supposed to be banned from this place. Tony had assured him of the impenetrable security.

He glanced back over his shoulder. There the leeches were, three guys with cameras pointing them in the direction of the blonde actress. Unfortunately, Alexia and he, although behind the actress, were in their line of sight.

"Clearly, we do need to talk."

Only moments too late, the club's bouncers strode through the crowd toward the cameramen. Barbie and her entourage were shrieking in outrage, but Rafe got the feeling the outrage was as much an act as her last Oscar-nominated role.

Rafe looked down into wide green eyes belatedly filled with concern. He felt the press of breasts against his chest, felt Alexia's slender fragility within the circle of his arms. She was smaller than he'd realized, and shorter, even with her death-defying heels. The top of her head was tucked neatly beneath his chin.

He felt other things, things he shouldn't feel for his brother's proposed bride. The protectiveness was okay, it was the pleasure and possessiveness that bothered him. He told himself that they were almost automatic responses when he held a woman in his arms. It didn't mean anything except that he had to let her go. He loosed his hold on her, putting a safer distance between them.

One of the actress's party made a lunge for a photographer's camera. A punch was thrown, then another.

Rafe shepherded Alexia away from the tussle. Worry creased her forehead even as the bouncers quickly separated the opponents and dragged the guy who'd thrown the first punch away with the photographers.

"Do you think we're in the shots?" She bit her bottom lip.

At least she realized how it would look if pictures of the two of them in a nightclub, standing close, got into the papers at home. Or if they were implicated in the brawl, which, given the way the press liked to play with the truth, wouldn't surprise him in the least. The public of San Philippe would be curious. Adam would be furious. And if anything happened to jeopardize his father's plans, Rafe would be in the firing line. He just needed to get this one simple job done. Get Alexia back to San Philippe—without a scandal—and wash his hands of her. How hard could it be?

He shook his head. "I'm scarcely known here, and you, fortunately, hardly look like yourself. Even if we're in the background, they weren't after us. We'll be cropped out."

"Fortunately?"

"Don't sound offended. You deliberately tried to

disguise yourself. For good reason. So, yes, fortunately."
He didn't add that in other respects it was most *un*for-
tunate. The figure-hugging dress, her long legs, the
satiny skin of her arms, the curl of her lashes, her scent.
All most unfortunate. Where was the boring—safe—
Alexia? "How did you get here?" His question sounded
harsher than he meant it to.

"Motorbike," she answered, with a glimmer of
defiance.

He hid his surprise. "You rode?" That had been her
on the bike?

Her chin lifted. "With Mario."

"In that dress?" He had a sudden vision of the dress
riding high up a creamy expanse of thigh.

"I changed at a friend's apartment."

He looked at Mario. The other man moved closer.
"Take the bike home."

Mario nodded.

"Where'd you get him, anyway?" he asked as they
watched Mario's departing back.

"He's one of our drivers. He also has security,
bodyguard-type training. And he's the best dancer of
the firm's drivers."

Rafe glared at her. "Undoubtedly a reliable way
to choose your security for the evening." He silently
counted the hours—eighteen—till they'd be safely back
in San Philippe and he'd be done with her.

Lexie sat quietly as they drove in the muted silence
of Rafe's Aston Martin to the Wyndham Joneses'
estate. Why him? She'd encountered good friends at

the nightclub before who'd failed to recognize her. And yet Rafe, whom she'd met only a handful of times, had known her.

The purpose and urgency that had infused him as he'd all but picked her up and bundled her into his car had gone. He drove the powerful machine with relaxed effortlessness, his hands curled lightly around the distinctive three-spoked steering wheel. But she sensed his underlying tension, and it was in her interests to placate him. She wanted him to see that she really was suitable for his brother. Serene, regal, dignified.

"Nice car." She smoothed her palms over the soft black leather of her seat.

He said nothing.

"It's a Vantage, isn't it? A V12?" She exhausted her knowledge of the car.

"I wouldn't know." His usually undetectable accent, foreign and vaguely French, colored his words.

So much for getting him to relax by complimenting his car. It worked on most men she knew. His dismissiveness needled her. He'd clearly made up his mind not to engage with her. "A real playboy car."

That drew her a scornful look, at least.

"How'd you get it, anyway?"

"My secretary arranged it. Ask him."

Lexie gave up trying to either soothe or bait him and looked out her window at the city and then countryside sliding by. Gone. Soon she'd be gone from here and the narrow confines of her life.

As the estate gates closed behind them, he pulled off

the driveway into a wooded area. The house was still half a mile away.

"Why are we stopping here?"

"Because if I don't stop till we're in front of the house someone will doubtless come out and find me with my hands wrapped around your neck. And while I'm sure whoever it is will sympathize with me, it'd still be frowned upon, bound to cause a diplomatic fracas. And worse, I'll be interrupted."

He'd had a hand around the back of her neck once four years ago as he'd kissed her senseless. Which was not what she should be remembering now. She called up righteous anger. "You're assuming you'll get the chance to wrap your hands around my neck. If you'd read my background information—" which of course the Playboy Prince wouldn't have "—you'd know I have a black belt in karate. Second dan." She was tired of him thinking he could push her around. "Perhaps it'd be my hands around *your* neck."

Unfortunately, a contrary image sprang to mind of the two of them in the car with their hands all over each other in a very different way. Shocked at herself, she banished the image. It had only happened because he reminded her of Adam and they were confined in the intimacy of his car, faces and bodies close, emotions running high. The scent of his cologne, masculine and appealing, wasn't helping, either.

He laughed, low and deep. "I did read the information. My secretary handed it to me as I boarded the jet, and unfortunately there was nothing else on board to read. It mentioned years of ballet dancing, sailing and show jumping to a nationally competitive level, and musical accomplishments including flute and, rather more surprising, the saxophone. Sadly, they must have left off the karate. Though it's entirely possible that the ballet training will help in the execution of a passable roundhouse kick."

Lexie knew when to quit. He clearly wasn't going to fall for that one. Even if she had learned karate. Once. A long time ago. A secret rebellion cut short.

He turned off the engine. And though she'd scarcely heard the car's low purr before, the silence of the night settled over them like a heavy, uncomfortable blanket.

Now it was just her and Rafe.

He turned, filling the space in the suddenly too-small car from floor to ceiling, his presence surrounding her. Just enough light washed in from the closest of the lamps dotted along the driveway to make out his features, the dark brows drawn together, the strong nose, surprisingly full lips and the stubborn, stubborn jaw. And the eyes that raked disrespectfully over her. Adam would never have looked at her like that.

"Your headache is better, I take it?"

"Much, thank you." She chose to ignore the drawled sarcasm. And the lie of her fabricated illness.

"You often pull stunts like that, Precious?"

"I don't pull stunts. I wanted to go out tonight. I wanted to dance. There's no crime in it."

"It was a stunt. And it was stupid."

"It was not stupid. I was careful. I took Mario with me." Her life was about to change; all she'd wanted was one night of anonymity. It wasn't so much to ask. She'd been to the nightclub before. Many times. And in all that time she'd never been recognized.

"And look what happened."

"Nothing happened." He'd said himself they wouldn't turn up in those shots.

"Do you have any idea— Damn." He sat back in his seat.

"What?"

"I sound like my father." His hand clenched into a fist. "I can't believe it."

That concept apparently bothered him almost as much as the nightclub debacle had because he lapsed into silence. "How did you know I was at the nightclub?" she asked. "Did you follow me?"

"No. A happy coincidence."

"Not my definition of happy." At that he smiled. "So you were there, too," she accused, "for the same reason as me, and yet I'm the one in the wrong?"

"I'm not the one who left dinner early because—" he touched blunt fingertips to his temple and blinked several times, a parody of a woman fluttering her eyelashes "—I had a headache."

"I did have a headache. That dinner would have given a saint one. I never said what I was going to do about it. If you assumed I was retiring quietly to my bed, that's not my fault."

"If you want to be wife to the crown prince, you're going to need a little more fortitude. It'll be your job to stay at dinners like that till the bitter end. You weren't the only one who wanted to leave that dinner tonight. Some of us managed to tough it out."

"That's it?" She smiled with a sudden flash of insight. "You're sore that I got to leave earlier than you?"

"That's not what I said. The problem wasn't with you leaving the dinner, headache or not. It lies more in you out with other men, dancing the way you were."

"There was nothing wrong with the way I danced."

"No? Every man in the place enjoyed it."

She felt the stab of his criticism. "You are being so unfair."

Rafe turned back to stare out the windshield. "Maybe. But you need to learn how very important appearances are. How very seriously people—like Adam—take them."

The worst of it was that he was right. She'd been brought up to always consider how anything she did, said, wore might look. Her mother was as hyperaware of appearances as anyone Lexie had ever met. Which made her occasional forays to the nightclub so liberating. So exhilarating.

She hadn't planned on Adam ever knowing. "It might have been my last chance," she said quietly, leaning back in her seat, and that was the truth of it.

"You're right about that. But no one's forcing you to come to San Philippe."

She said nothing.

"Are they?"

She met his steady gaze. "No." This was her choice. She'd dreamed of it for so long.

"This arrangement is far from a done deal, Alexia," he said quietly. "I'll be watching you, and if I find out you're using Adam, that on your side the relationship is a pretence, I'll hustle your duplicitous derriere back home so fast you won't know what hit you."

"*Duplicitous derriere* sounds so much better than *my lying ass*. Or *hypocrite*." She gave the last word emphasis because it could apply just as well to him. "You won't catch me out because there's nothing to catch me out in." She turned to stare out the window at the darker silhouettes of trees shadowing the night. "How sweet for Adam to have you coming to his assistance."

"Adam doesn't know women the way I do."

"I wouldn't choose to have any kind of a relationship with him if he did." Adam was serious and constant as well as kind. Nothing like the man sitting a hand span away from her radiating cynicism and testosterone.

"He doesn't look for subterfuge."

"But you do?" She almost felt sorry for him. "Must make for interesting relationships for you. Ever heard of trust?"

"All I'm saying is that if Adam and San Philippe are what you really want, don't screw it up."

"Don't screw it up?" Lexie's knee bumped against the gear stick as she pivoted in her seat. "That's a little rich coming from you, isn't it? I thought you were the 'Prince of Screw-Ups.'" One tabloid had, in fact, tried to pin that label on Rafe. It hadn't stuck, but Lexie suspected that was only because it lacked originality or alliteration.

"Don't try to make this about me." His voice was cold, as though she'd hit a nerve.

"Well, don't try to sully the relationship Adam and I have."

. A look of scorn passed across his face. "A few letters and e-mails do not constitute a relationship."

"They constitute more of a relationship than gratuitous sex, which if the stories about you are to be believed—"

"They're not."

His vehemence silenced her.

"And even if they were, the difference, Precious, is that my business is no concern of yours. Whereas your business is my concern. At least until I get you back to San Philippe and offload you onto Adam."

"Offload me?"

"Wrong word, sorry." His offhand apology only incensed her further.

"No, it wasn't. Offload me is exactly what you meant. I'll save you the trouble for tonight." She'd had more than enough of his company for one evening. Opening her door, she climbed out and stalked down the driveway. The cool night air was the perfect antidote to the tension in the car, and she forced herself to take deep, calming breaths. Behind her, a car door shut. Moments later, the engine purred to life, the car eased alongside her, and the window slid down. "Get in. I'll drive you."

"I'm walking, so you may as well stop following me. Consider me offloaded."

"Don't be ridiculous."

"Ridiculous?"

He made no pretence this time that he'd used the wrong word. "Yes. Childishly ridiculous."

Lexie clenched her jaw and walked faster, then stumbled in the high strappy sandals, which were fine for the smooth dance floor, but definitely weren't made for striding on driveways. The low rumble of masculine laughter sounded from within the car.

She stopped and whirled to face him, then bent to take off her shoes, tossing them one at a time through the car window and onto the seat beside him. She pulled off the wig too, and it followed her shoes into his car.

As her hair unfurled around her shoulders, his smile suddenly disappeared. She turned and, ignoring his call to her, darted into the lightly wooded area bordering the driveway. She'd grown up here, had played, whenever she'd been allowed to escape, amongst these very trees. Some of those times of escape had even been at night. A girl took her freedom where she could. She scarcely needed the occasional shafts of light that filtered through from the driveway lamps.

She caught a sound behind her and stilled, alert and listening, her senses heightened. "Alexia." Her name sounded on the night, low and clear. "Cut this out and come back to the car. Now."

He was not happy. Lexie smiled. "Or what? You'll make me? I don't think so, Rafe."

His silence was ominous.

Lexie's heart beat faster. "I'm fine." She slipped behind a tree. "You drive. I'll make my own way." She darted for another tree, stopped and listened again.

She heard nothing, but caught the faintest trace of his cologne. He was close. She waited in the deepest shadows she could find, her shoulder pressed against the roughened bark of an ancient oak, and held herself perfectly still, kept her breathing quiet and even.

From behind, a strong hand clamped around her arm, and without thought a scream started in the back of her throat. The hand swept up to gently cover her mouth, cutting off the incipient sound. She was pulled back against a broad chest. "Do not scream." The softened command was spoken clearly into her ear. "It's only me—" his breath was warm on her skin "—and the very last thing we need tonight is for security to come."

She swallowed and nodded. The hand lowered from her mouth, but she was still clamped against that broad chest. It was the second time in the space of an hour she'd been pressed against its hard contours. It didn't feel like the body she would have expected from the profligate prince. Sure, he was tall and lean. She'd figured that build, combined with the occasional gym workout and exceptional tailoring, was enough to give the fine line to the clothes he wore. But the chest and the arms about her spoke of sinew and strength and an intimidating elemental toughness that was eons away from the high life he lived.

"How did you find me?"

"I've done my share of nighttime operations." His arms loosened and he stepped away from her. "You, Precious, were a piece of cake."

Of course. All men in San Philippe, including the princes, served two years in the armed forces. Rafe, from memory, had served even longer, spending time in each of the three military services.

"Now we're going back to the car." She heard the carefully reined-in temper beneath his quiet words. "And we're going to the house."

She nodded again. It was definitely time to get the willful streak she'd worked so hard to conquer back under control. She was achieving nothing letting Rafe goad her. "I was going anyway. Once I'd cooled off." Which she'd done now, emotionally and physically. She suppressed a shiver.

As they turned for the car, a jacket, warmed with the heat of Rafe's body and imbued with his subtle masculine scent, came to rest on her shoulders. The silk lining caressed the bare skin of her arms.

"Covering me up?"

"Warming you up. I personally have no problem with a little skin. But I will have a problem with my father and my brother if I take you back sick."

"Chivalrous to the end."

Unexpected, Rafe's rich, deep chuckle sounded on the air, eroding her resentment and warming her, against her will, as much as his jacket.

But the resentment was back in full force by the time Lexie reached her bedroom. She shut the door, leaned against it for a second, then crossed to a window and looked out along the shadowy driveway. The driveway, which, after insisting she come back to his car, Rafe had made her walk down. Well, not "make" exactly, but he'd somehow made it seem the only option for her pride. Another besetting sin to add to her list.

He'd idled along beside her, occasionally offering her a ride. She'd refused with the line about not getting into cars with strange men, which had drawn out that unexpected laughter again. In reality the only strange thing about him was the heat—the temper—he ignited in her. He'd talked a little about the car, the ergonomic design, the comfort of the heated leather seats, proving either that he'd lied when he pretended to know nothing about it or that he was lying now as he made up features.

As soon as she reached the house, she'd gone in, leaving him to drive around to the garage and make his own way. Army boy should have no problems with that. Unfortunately.

She sat in front of her dresser and brushed out her hair. Apparently, the hundred strokes a night that Maria, her live-in nanny for the first ten years of her life, had insisted on had been disproved as doing any real good, but sometimes it was just so therapeutic. Lexie caught her flushed reflection in the mirror and made herself take a deep, slow breath.

If only it had been Adam who'd come for her, this mess wouldn't be unraveling in her hands. She'd be the woman she was supposed to be. She would have stayed by his side for the dinner. She would have stayed in for the night. She would have had nothing to do with Rafe.

Twenty-seven, twenty-eight. Of all people, why Rafe? *Twenty- nine, thirty.* Why had he come to that same nightclub? Why had he recognized her? And more important, why did she let him make her feel so inept and inadequate and infuriated? "The arrogant, inconsiderate, hypocritical, condescending...prude."

A shape moved in the mirror behind her and she whirled to face it, her hairbrush raised. Rafe stood a few feet away, eyeing her choice of weapon with scarcely concealed amusement. "I did knock. You were talking so loudly you didn't hear me." She lowered the brush, turned back to the mirror and started brushing again. *Thirty-one, thirty-two.*

"I've definitely had arrogant and inconsiderate before," he said thoughtfully, moving a little closer. "I don't *think* I've been called hypocritical or condescending, at least not to my face. But I'm absolutely positive I've never been called a prude."

Lexie studied his reflection. His white shirt lay open at the collar, revealing a vee of tanned skin and reminding her that she still wore his jacket, the too-long sleeves pushed carelessly up. Stubble darkened his jaw. Her sandals dangled from one hand, looking ridiculously flimsy in his grip. In the other hand he held her wig. Behind him, her big bed, the covers turned back, her lacy nightgown laid out, filled the background.

She dragged her gaze away from him, focusing on her own reflection and brushing her hair. "Look at what you're wearing," she said, mimicking his voice. "The people of San Philippe are very conservative, Alexia." She spoke to him in her mirror. "And the way you dance. Sounded prudish to me."

A smile, not in the least prudish, played about his lips and eyes, threatening to distract her. "So? Prudish?" She nodded. "And hypocritical?"

She held tight to her anger, wouldn't let herself be beguiled by the charm he could wield. "I've read about you on the Internet. Seen pictures." She knew about his latest, brief affair. He shifted uncomfortably, his expression clouding. "I'm practically Amish in comparison to you. And I've been to San Philippe more than once—it's not that different from here in terms of conservatism." She waited for his response.

"Finished? You don't want to expound on arrogant and inconsiderate?"

"Self-explanatory, I would have thought." She wanted to point out just how inconsiderate he'd been, making her walk, but that had kind of been her fault. Still, she was paying for it now; the soles of her feet were stinging. She'd probably have been better off keeping the four-inch heels on.

"I can accept some of your points."

Not used to the people in her life admitting mistakes, she hid her surprise.

"And you're right, not everyone in San Philippe is conservative. But I'll tell you one person who most definitely is."

She sighed and put her brush down. "Adam?"

He nodded.

"It's one of the things I like about him. It seems sweet and noble." Unlike his brother, there had never been a hint of scandal attached to Adam.

"He's noble. He's not sweet." Rafe walked closer. The description seemed to fit him just as well. There was nobility in his bearing, his aristocratic features, and nothing sweet about the hard glaze to his eyes. He stopped at her side, heat radiating from him as he lowered her wig to the dresser. It lay like a small, sleek animal. His fingers, large and blunt, traced the length of the dark hair. And for a second she recalled how those fingers had felt the time he had plunged them into her hair. How he had cradled her head for the erotic assault of his kiss. She quickly turned her eyes back to the mirror.

He dropped her shoes to the carpet. And still he stood there, making it difficult for her to breathe normally.

"We want the same thing here, Alexia." His gaze tracked to her hair, her real hair. He lifted his hand and ran his thumb and forefinger down the length of a lock before frowning, clenching his hand into a fist and lowering it to his side. "We both want to get you to San Philippe as soon as possible. And without any scandal. Don't we?"

"Yes, of course." Lexie swallowed. "Can I point out that you being in my room at 3:00 a.m. is probably not the best way to go about that?"

"Probably not."

She waited for him to move. And waited. "If you're finished, I guess you can go."

"One more thing."

Surprising her for the second time that night, even more than the first, he crouched before her and, wrapping his fingers around her ankle, picked up her foot, lifting it so he could see the sole. He ran his forefinger along the arch. "How is it?"

Ignoring the response to his touch that seemed to slither from her sole and up along her leg, Lexie swallowed. "Fine."

A corner of Rafe's mouth quirked up. "I don't suppose it is. But you'll live." He placed her foot carefully back down on the plush carpet, picked up her other foot and, after running his thumb along the sensitive underside of that one, too, placed it back beside the first.

Lexie stood as he straightened and turned to go. "Your jacket." If she got rid of that there would be no link between them from tonight.

He moved behind her. As she shrugged the jacket from her shoulders he slipped his hands beneath her hair to grasp the collar, his knuckles skimming her neck. Her eyes met his in the mirror as he drew the garment down her arms. For a second their gazes locked. It was as though he was undressing her and she was allowing it. Sudden heat suffused her, coalescing deep inside her. Lexie closed her eyes so he wouldn't be able to read her response, part confusion and part desire.

Three

Lexie paused with her cup of strong black coffee halfway to her lips as Rafe strolled onto the terrace where her mother and the dozen or so guests who'd stayed over last night had gathered for breakfast. She put her cup down and followed his progress. He was immaculate, gorgeous. Even the sun seemed to brighten with his entrance, sparkling on the nearby lake.

It shouldn't annoy her that he looked so good and so relaxed. But it did.

He approached their table. Lexie's only comfort was that the four seats were already taken. "Antonia." He smiled at her mother, a flash of white perfect teeth, warmth in his eyes. "Clayton, Jackson," he greeted the two elderly oilmen already at her table.

Finally, deliberately, his gaze found hers. "Alexia." He

dipped his head, no trace of remembrance of that other gaze, the one that had heated her very being. No wonder women fell over themselves for him, she'd thought as she'd lain in bed, sleep slowly claiming her.

"Rafe." She nodded back, found a smile in her repertoire, hoped it was both gracious and remote.

Lexie returned her attention to Clayton. But still she was aware of Rafe as he strolled to the side table where breakfast was laid out and picked up a plate. She'd expected, hoped, he would sleep in. Wasn't that what indolent playboy princes did? Except she was having a difficult time seeing him fit so neatly into that role anymore. There was something about the ease with which he'd found her in the darkness and the steel of the body she'd twice been pressed against, the uncompromising strength of the arms that had held her. Something about the standards he wanted her to uphold, and his discomfort and displeasure when she'd mentioned his scandals.

Clayton wiped his mouth with his napkin. "I'll thank you lovely ladies for your hospitality." He addressed both her and her mother.

"You're not going?" Lexie asked, appalled.

"I'm afraid so." He smiled as he pushed back his chair, flattered by her clear disappointment.

Jackson stood too. "Likewise, ma'am."

"Surely you'll have another cup of coffee." Lexie tried to keep the desperation from her voice. She wasn't ready to face Rafe again, and if there were vacant seats at her table she just knew he'd sit there.

"Love to," Clayton said, "but the doc's told me to cut

back. Thanks again." And then they were both gone, and the housekeeper, always efficient, swept in and cleared away their plates.

Lexie, atoning for her early exit from dinner, had promised her mother she'd stay till all the guests had breakfasted. Otherwise she would have been hot on Clayton's and Jackson's heels.

She looked down at her barely touched bowl of fruit salad and yogurt and began a mental countdown. *Ten, nine*...almost exactly as she hit zero the chair opposite her was drawn out. By the time she'd readied herself and looked up, Rafe was seated and watching her.

"How was your run?" her mother asked him.

He'd been for a run already? Lexie hid her surprise. She often ran in the mornings herself, but not when she'd had only a few hours' sleep. This morning she had barely dragged herself out of bed in time to dress properly for breakfast, and had done it only because it was so important to her mother. She stabbed a cube of melon in her bowl. *Who's the indolent one now?* a little voice taunted.

"Pleasant," he said in that deep, cultured voice. "You have lovely grounds, especially that wooded area that the driveway cuts through."

He was looking at her mother, but Lexie couldn't pull her gaze from him. What was he going to say next? Why bring up the scene of their midnight cat-and-mouse game? An incident that now, in the broad light of day, seemed almost surreal.

"Thank you. And you slept well last night?"

Lexie held her breath. Would he feel compelled out of

a misplaced sense of either responsibility or mischief to mention what had happened last night, how and where he'd found her? She was leaving today. She didn't need a lecture from her mother as a parting gift.

Rafe's knowing gaze met hers before transferring back to her mother. "Deeply."

But briefly, she thought, as she let her breath out on a sigh of relief and begrudging gratitude. She took aim at a strawberry with her fork. Even without going for a run, she'd managed only a few hours' sleep. In response to the thought, her jaw tensed with the beginnings of a yawn.

"I'm afraid you must find our country ways quite dull?" Antonia smiled at Rafe, and Lexie cringed. If only her mother would stop fishing for compliments.

Lexie looked up and caught the gleam in his dark eyes, and the urge to yawn disappeared. The fork stilled in her hand as she waited for his answer.

"On the contrary," he said easily, just as her mother would have expected. "Last night was fascinating. Far more interesting than I could have anticipated." Double meaning laced his words, and Lexie waited for her mother to pick up on it and probe further.

If only she would go and chat with some of the other guests. Lexie hadn't thought that after last night she could want to be alone with Rafe, but it would undoubtedly be better than this agony of trepidation.

"I'm delighted you thought so. I do have a reputation for the best dinner parties." Fortunately, her mother, while socially astute, could also be shallow. And for once Lexie found herself grateful for that fact. Her mother had no idea that Rafe could be talking about anything other than the dinner party and truly had no idea how dull the dinner had been in the first place. If people complimented her, which they always did, it was usually because of her wealth and status. She had to know that, it was how she thought, too. Her mother just couldn't quite believe it worked in reverse.

Lexie took a bite of her strawberry and forced herself to chew, pretending to concentrate on a breakfast that she was too anxious and too tired to really be interested in. She watched with something like envy and a little irritation as Rafe started on a plate of bacon and eggs.

She ate enough that it wouldn't look as if she was running from him before she pushed her bowl away a little. She was about to stand when her mother beat her to it, saying, "I really must have a word with Bill before he leaves, I've been sadly ignoring him." And then she was gone. Lexie could hardly go now, too, and leave Rafe sitting alone at the table. Gritting her teeth, she reached for her orange juice.

"Don't stay on my account, Precious," he murmured, apparently aware of her conflict. His knowing eyes watched her over the rim of his coffee cup. A hint of a grin taunted her.

Lexie folded her hands in her lap. "Thank you for not mentioning the nightclub to my mother."

He sat back a little. "You didn't seriously think I would? What you do or don't tell your mother is no concern of mine."

"Thank you anyway."

As he shrugged off her thanks his cell phone rang.

He pulled it from his pocket and, frowning, glanced at the caller ID. "Excuse me. It's my brother. I need to take it." He stood and strolled off the terrace.

What she told her mother might be no concern of his, but what he told his brother was surely an entirely different matter. She hadn't done anything to be ashamed of, but it would still be better if she was the one to mention it to Adam.

If it needed mentioning at all.

She could hear nothing of his conversation as he walked away. He passed Stanley, who stood to one side of the terrace overseeing the proceedings, and disappeared from sight behind a manicured hedge.

Grasping what was possibly her last opportunity to talk to her old friend, she picked up her coffee cup and made her way over to the butler. If she was also closer to Rafe, it was purely coincidence.

"Pleasant evening last night, miss?" he asked, a twinkle in his eye.

"Not you, too?" Stanley was the only one in the household who knew about her love of dancing and her occasional nightclub escapes.

"Meaning?"

"I got busted."

"By?" His concern showed in that single syllable.

"The Frog Prince."

The concern deepened. "He wasn't impressed?"

"Ah, no, that's not how I'd describe his reaction."

As Stanley allowed a smile, her mother's laughter reached them, and they both looked in her direction.

"Clearly, he didn't feel obliged to mention it to your mother."

"No. Thankfully. At least not yet, anyway."

"I'm sure he's the last person who would."

Stanley, too, knew of Rafe's reputation. But despite Rafe's assurances, and his own not infrequent misdemeanors, Lexie wasn't one hundred percent certain that Rafe wouldn't use his information to her detriment if he felt it served his purpose, either here or in San Philippe. "You're probably right," she said, at least partially to reassure herself.

"One other thing," Stanley said.

"Yes?"

"You might want to stop calling him the Frog Prince, if he's to become your brother-in-law."

"I know," she said on a sigh.

"You don't have to go."

Lexie looked back at the breakfast table, the assembled guests, her mother presiding over it all, and quashed her own doubts. "I know you think what I'm doing is crazy. And sometimes I think that, too, because it doesn't always make sense. But I want to go. I love San Philippe. I can't explain why, but I've always felt welcome and at home there. And of course there's Adam." Maybe he shouldn't have been last on that list.

"Dammit, Adam," Rafe's voice carried suddenly to her. "Shouldn't you be the one to do that with her?" His pacing had brought him to the other side of the topiaried hedge. She couldn't see him because the hedge made a dense screen, but it was far from soundproof. "Logically, yes, but—" He walked a little farther off. "I have a life to get back to." Lexie still heard his words, and she was fairly sure she was the topic of conversation. "I have better things to do with my time than babysitting or running your errands for you." Now she was definitely sure, and a weight settled in her stomach. "This whole situation is ludicrous." Rafe's disdain for her was clear. "I can't imagine what sort of scheming or hopelessly naive woman would—"

Stanley cleared his throat. "On the other hand," he said, talking over Rafe's voice, "the Frog Prince has a certain ring to it."

Lexie laughed, but the sound was brittle. That was the closest she'd ever heard Stanley come to criticizing anyone, and she knew he'd done it for her.

She shouldn't let anything Rafe said cut her; he was surely the last person whose approval she needed or wanted, but still, his words, and the contempt in them, had hurt. Had sullied her dream.

A few overheard words and suddenly she was questioning not just her plans, but her very nature. Scheming or naive? Was that how Rafe and perhaps Adam saw her? Could she be either of those things? She knew she was idealistic—but that didn't make her naive, did it? And she was halfway in love with Adam, and wanted to fall the rest of the way and to have him fall in love with her—did that make her scheming?

She looked again in Rafe's direction. He'd walked round the edge of the hedge. His brows were drawn together, as though in hearing her laughter he'd perhaps realized that he, too, could be heard. He turned away, and Lexie watched his departing back as, phone still pressed to his ear, he strode in the opposite direction.

With the sun beating down on him, Rafe waited by the limousine and flicked a glance at his watch. Ten minutes late. Her bags were already in the trunk of the car; it was just Precious herself who was missing. It was hot out here, and though he could wait in the relative comfort of either the house or the car, he had no desire to be cooped up any longer than he had to be. He looked again at the wide stairs to the house and finally, finally, the door opened and the butler walked out. The butler, but no Alexia. Rafe curbed his frustration. "Where is she?"

"Not in the house, sir." The butler had been well trained; his voice revealed absolutely nothing.

"Then where?"

"Most likely out riding. I checked with the stables and one of her horses is gone, though no one actually saw her leave. I'm afraid she sometimes loses track of time when she's riding."

Rafe shrugged out of his jacket and tossed it into the limo. "Show me these stables."

"You can go now." Rafe dismissed the groom who'd accompanied him this far, then urged his mount toward the woman sitting, hands linked around her knees, on a log at the shore of the lake. Behind her, a tethered bay mare cropped the grass. With the sunlight catching on her hair, she made a picture as beautiful as any he'd seen at any of the hundreds of galleries he'd opened or visited. But something about the stillness with which she held herself and the droop to her shoulders filled him with foreboding. She looked alone and weighted with worry, or sorrow…or regret?

As he'd ridden he'd been prepared to tear strips off her when he found her. But at the sight of her his anger dissipated. He'd never been any good at holding on to that particular emotion anyway. Life was for living and was too short to waste being angry.

Leaving his horse tethered near hers, he sat beside her on the log, their shoulders almost touching. He looked at her booted feet, recalled their slender vulnerability as he'd touched them last night.

"I'm sorry," she said quietly. Her fingers were so tightly interlaced they were white.

"Don't worry. This isn't the first time I've been kept waiting by a woman." Though he knew that wasn't what her heartfelt apology had been for. "The third, I think. Although both of the others were by my sister." A curtain of auburn hair, lusher even than he'd realized last night, partially obscured her face, but he caught a rewarding glimmer of a smile before it vanished. "It doesn't matter. Private jet. It's hardly going to go without us."

"I can't go."

His foreboding deepened and settled heavily in his stomach. He had to get her back to San Philippe. "Of course you can. Everything's ready. Your cases are in the car. The pilot's one of our best. Hardly ever crashes." He tucked her hair behind her ear and searched for her smile, but found nothing.

"You were right. This whole situation is ludicrous. No normal person would have agreed to it. I've just been so caught up in the dream I never really stopped to think about it."

Ahh. So she had heard that. "Alexia, I seldom take anything seriously, so you shouldn't take anything I say seriously, either." Certainly his family knew better than to do that. "You've had a crush on Adam for years, right?"

She nodded. "Since I was twelve."

"Wow." He hadn't thought it had been that long. He'd realized the night four years ago when she'd kissed him with that odd combination of passion and melting innocence, thinking he was Adam, that she'd imagined she had feelings for his brother.

"Stupid, huh?"

Privately, he agreed with the sentiment. Adam had at the time been much taken by the ambassador's daughter, a woman of sultry beauty with ten years on Alexia in age and a lifetime in sophistication. And even now, as far as Rafe could tell, his brother was agreeing to this "courtship" primarily out of a sense of duty. "You can't help what you feel."

"Although I think it might even have started when I was eight and you threw that frog in my lap, and Adam caught it and took it away."

Rafe smiled. "Arthur."

"Arthur?"

"The frog."

She turned her face to him, curious. "He was a pet?"

Fourteen years later and he could probably still tell

her a dozen facts about Arthur and his kind. She'd certainly be more receptive to them now than she was when she was eight, particularly given how eager she was not to have the discussion they should be having. "Let's get back to Adam, your knight in shining armor. Saving the damsel in distress. Rescuing you from evil amphibians."

"He doesn't feel anything for me."

"*Now* this is bothering you?" That earned him a small, sheepish smile. "Give him a chance. He doesn't know you. I think he'll like you." He didn't add that his father had practically ordered it.

"Do you really?" She turned toward him, all earnestness.

He looked at her pale, beautiful face, hair that begged a man to sink his hands into it, a figure he could still recall the imprint of against him.

Something of his thoughts must have shown. "I'm talking personalities here," she added. A twinkle of mischief lit her eyes.

She had strength and humor to go with her beauty. "Yes, I do think he'll like you. You might even still like him once you get to know him. But neither of you will know unless you give yourselves a chance. You'll regret it if you don't go. And if it doesn't work, you haven't lost anything."

If he went back to San Philippe without her, the blame would be laid squarely at his feet. And the likely punishment would be fighting off his own wedding. Heaven only knew who his father had in mind for him, though he'd undoubtedly have someone. He hadn't asked—that would only encourage the old man.

"Except maybe a little bit of pride."

"Pride, schmide, there's more than enough of that to go round."

"I do always enjoy visiting San Philippe. It's funny, but I feel at home there, I get a kind of déjà vu, like it's where I belong. More so than here even."

"That settles it then. Let's go." He was about to stand when she stilled him with her delicate hand on his forearm.

"Thank you. I'm not usually indecisive. It helped. Talking to you."

Unaccountably aware of her touch, wanting to take that hand in his own and lift it again to his lips, he instead stood. "Don't thank me, Alexia. I'm looking out for my interests as much as yours. There'd be no end of drama if I went home without you."

"Thank you anyway. It helped."

Rafe shrugged off her gratitude. "Anytime." Unlike with Adam, people didn't often turn to him for advice. And he didn't often dispense it. Didn't want that responsibility. But if he'd helped her he was glad of it. It meant he was one step closer to getting rid of her.

She looked at him, her green eyes bright and innocent and hopeful. "My friends call me Lexie."

Sexy Lexie. The epithet slid into his head. And she was sexy, in a way she seemed totally unaware of. It was her hair and those smiling, softly parted lips. And that was without even starting on her body. For the first time he could remember, Rafe almost envied Adam.

Oh, yeah. He definitely needed to get rid of her.

Experiencing his own sense of déjà vu, Rafe waited by the limousine. She'd said she needed just twenty minutes to change and be ready. Rafe knew a woman's twenty minutes, and he was prepared to wait. He looked up at the double front doors just as Alexia—he wouldn't let himself think of her as Lexie, because he couldn't help but rhyme it with "sexy"—stepped out, the family's butler at her side. Together they descended the stairs. She was doing the boring thing again, with her hair drawn back from her face, its auburn lushness fiercely constrained. She wore a cream suit with a beige top beneath the buttoned-up jacket and a single strand of pearls around her neck.

She stopped at his side. "Let's go, then."

"Your mother?" Who knew how long she'd be or what kind of production she'd make over her daughter's leaving.

"She's at a luncheon for the Historical Society."

Who knew indeed? Apparently, no production at all, or none more than the touching speech at dinner last night. One he'd thought at the time seemed more for the benefit of the guests than Alexia herself. Rafe understood duty and commitments better than most, but he would have thought.... It didn't matter. It was no business of his.

"We said goodbye earlier," she explained, and he

wasn't sure if the explanation was for his benefit or her own.

Their driver held open the door of the dark Bentley. Rafe waited for her to get in. Instead, she turned and enveloped the butler in a fierce hug.

"Take care, miss," the man murmured.

"I will, Stanley. You, too."

"Of course."

As Alexia was planting her neat behind in the car, Stanley turned to Rafe. "Look after her. Please."

Never in his life had he been given a command by a butler, and despite the added "please" it most definitely had been a command. But the moisture in the older man's eyes persuaded Rafe to let it pass. "Of course." Given the absence of her mother, he was glad she at least had someone who seemed to care about her.

Rafe eased into the limo, picked up the newspaper that lay on the seat between them, and scanned the headlines. Alexia was silent as the car eased along the driveway, silent as they passed the wooded area he'd found her in last night, silent as the gates swung closed behind them.

Finally, he looked at her, expecting to see a resurgence of her regret, prepared, this time, to bury his nose in the paper. She was here now and couldn't back out. Instead, the look of exhilaration on her face stole his breath away. She turned and caught him staring. If anything, her wide smile broadened.

"No more second thoughts, I take it."

"If I'm going, then I'm going to enjoy it. No point doing something halfheartedly." She glanced back over her shoulder. "Besides, you have no idea of the sense of freedom those gates shutting behind me for the last time gives me."

"Clearly."

She was still smiling. "Okay, maybe you do. But still."

"You were free to come and go, weren't you?"

"Yes. More or less. It's just different. I wouldn't expect you to understand."

"It may not be my place to break it to you, but if you're expecting freedom in signing up to join a royal family, you're sadly mistaken."

"But if…"

He waited.

"If it does work out with Adam, I'll be with a wonderful man, I'll be mistress of my own house, my own life."

It didn't escape him that she'd omitted to mention she'd also be married to the heir apparent to the San Philippe throne. How much did the cachet of that role weigh with her? "I guess," he said. "But have you seen the schedule arranged for you? From memory there are banquets, state dinners, garden shows, the anniversary parade and fireworks, a christening. The list goes on and on." She'd be on the go from the minute they touched down.

"Yes. I've seen it." She shrugged. "I like to be busy."

Which reminded him of the first amendment to that schedule. "By the way. You know we're not heading straight to San Philippe?"

"Yes."

"Adam spoke to you?"

"Just after he spoke to you, I believe."

After he'd been so tactless and careless as to allow her to overhear him. "And you're…okay with that?"

"Stopping in London, or—"

"I meant the jewelry thing." Somehow, he was taking Adam's prospective fiancée jewelry shopping for the earrings Adam wanted to give her, or that Adam's advisers had suggested he give her.

"It's sweet that Adam wants me to pick something out."

Sweet. Right. "And you don't mind that—"

"What?"

"Nothing." It was none of his business.

"That he's making you do it with me?"

If Rafe wanted to give a woman jewelry, especially a woman like Alexia, he'd pick something out himself, something with emeralds that sparkled like her eyes, or amber burnished with gold, like her hair, something a little unusual, unique even. A fire opal, lit from within. "It's no skin off my nose."

"I'm sure it is. And naturally I don't want to be an imposition to you. I understand that…you've got a life to live, but other than that—" again the smile, unfettered, joyous "—I couldn't be happier. Besides, I love London."

"We won't be there long. Just a few hours."

"And then you can offload me onto Adam." She said it with such a smile that he knew she wasn't still upset by his words, though the faux pas still irked him. He was better than that. Usually. It was just this whole thing with Alexia. He wanted no part of it.

Her gaze stayed on him, innocent and curious. "Do you have a girlfriend?"

The question, coming out of the blue, caught him by surprise. "No."

"What about—"

She was about to refer to the fiasco with his ex, Delilah. "That's over. It was over from the moment I found out she was married. Unfortunately, that was the moment I read it in the papers."

"You hadn't known?"

"She and her husband were having a trial separation. She neglected to mention his existence." Rafe was still angered by her deception, and even more annoyed at himself for being taken in by it. The media had had a field day with the story. Delilah had made a killing from selling her version of events to a prominent women's magazine.

"Did you love her?"

Rafe smiled. "No. Of course not."

"Oh."

She sounded so disappointed he almost laughed. "I don't do love. I don't even do serious. In case anyone else gets to thinking it's love."

He could see disappointment in her eyes. Her kind of naivety was exactly why he preferred to date older women. Women who knew the score. She had so much to learn, and there was a good chance she was going to get hurt in the process.

And he'd been the one to talk her into it.

Four

Lexie stood staring absently out the window at the fog shrouded London skyline. The fog lent the city an ethereal beauty, but it had closed the airport, necessitating an overnight stay.

A door shutting in the adjoining room alerted her to Rafe's return. The staff in his family's London apartments closed doors soundlessly, so it had to be him. He'd disappeared while the jewelers were still with her, leaving no indication of where he'd gone or when he'd be back. One of the staff had enquired as to whether she had any preferences for dinner and she had asked him to wait awhile. She'd been going to give Rafe another five minutes and then see about dinner for just herself, because she was ravenous. And if he didn't have the decency to tell her when, or even if, he was coming back, why should she wait?

She took a deep breath. Her emotions were all over the place—she knew that—fuelled by tiredness and anxiety. Her best course of action, she'd decided, was to remain aloof from him. Tomorrow they'd be in San Philippe and she would, she was certain, see very little of him. He, after all, had a life to live. A life she was currently interrupting.

And yet, for a few minutes as they'd sat together on the log yesterday morning, she'd imagined a connection with him. She realized now he'd just been doing what he deemed necessary to get her to come with him.

She turned as he entered the room, his long stride halting abruptly. The aura of tension that had shrouded him when he'd left had diminished, but not by much. He still radiated a barely contained, frustrated energy. It was there in the tightness of his jaw and shoulders, there in the depths of his eyes.

He didn't want to be stuck here. "The fog isn't my fault," she said in her defense. And more specifically he didn't want to be stuck here with *her*.

That much was clear from the way he tensed up around her. It would have been obvious even if she hadn't heard his phone call with Adam. He was watching her now, his steady gaze unreadable and disconcerting. "I'll be just as glad as you when we're on our way again. But in the meantime it'd certainly be a lot nicer if we could find a way to get along. And I know you don't owe me anything, but I'd appreciate it if you'd at least let me know whether or not to expect you back when you go out. So I know whether or not to eat without you."

The tension around his eyes had eased as she spoke, changing into surprised amusement. "Are you done?"

Amusement hadn't been the reaction she expected, and she sighed, realizing how petulant she'd sounded. Not in the least aloof. She had to fight not to respond to that warming humor in his eyes. "Yes," she said feeling more than a little foolish.

"And are you hungry?" he asked, a half grin lifting one corner of his lips.

"Yes." Her stomach grumbled audibly, confirming her answer. "And sometimes," she admitted, "I get a little cranky when I'm hungry."

"You don't say?" He was still trying to quell his grin. "And do you like pizza?"

Just the mention of her favorite fast food had her imagining she could smell it. "I love it," she said with possibly more enthusiasm than was appropriate, given the surprise that registered on Rafe's face. "Did that dossier on me go into that much detail?"

"What? About you getting cranky when you're hungry?" He was still grinning.

"No. About the pizza."

"No. Just asking. Hoping, actually."

At that moment, a liveried servant walked into the room carrying an incongruous-looking large, flat, cardboard box in his white-gloved hands. "The usual, sir?"

Rafe nodded.

Quickly, Rafe and the servant rearranged furniture so that two of the ornate and probably priceless dining chairs were placed in front of the wide window Lexie had recently been staring out of. An ottoman was set in front of the chairs and a side table between them.

The cardboard box, linen napkins, a bottle of pinot noir and two crystal goblets were placed on the side table.

As the servant left, Lexie glanced from the box to Rafe, and her stomach grumbled again. "Is that…?" The aroma of tomato and basil permeated the air.

Rafe smiled properly, looking inordinately proud of himself. "Sure is. The uncle of a friend of mine has a place not too far from here. He makes the best pizza outside of Italy." Rafe crossed to the table and folded back the lid of the box. "It's simple, but exquisite. And we don't have time for much else."

He gave a small bow and a theatrical sweep of his arm. "Take a seat, and help yourself."

They sat, feet almost touching on the ottoman, snow-white linen napkins on their laps, and ate looking out at the glowing lights of the fog-shrouded city.

For the first time in days the tension seeped from Lexie's shoulders and her breath slowed. She didn't speak until she'd finished her second slice of pizza. "Thank you. That was divine, and just what I needed."

"I figured it's going to be banquets from here on in till the end of the anniversary celebrations and that this might be…nice."

"It was better than nice. It was perfect."

The chimes of Big Ben rang out, carrying on the night air. Lexie took a sip of the pinot noir. "What did you mean, we don't have time for much else?"

Rafe glanced at his watch as he finished a mouthful

of pizza. From an inside pocket of his blazer he pulled a slip of paper and held it out to Lexie.

"What is it?"

"Look at it and find out."

She wiped her fingertips and took the paper, eyeing both Rafe and it suspiciously.

"Tickets," she ascertained quickly, then read the print, and then read it again. "Shakespeare. At the Globe." She stood, her napkin falling to the floor, and hugged the tickets to her chest. "I can't believe it. I didn't think there'd be any chance. I never even thought to ask."

"Royalty, even foreign and relatively minor, carries a certain amount of weight."

Lexie laughed with delight. "Thank you."

"Don't. I did it for both of us. It beats staying cooped up in these apartments all evening."

There was nothing *cooped up* about the expansive suites. But maybe to a prince? "Thank you, anyway. You have no idea how thrilled I am. I studied Shakespeare."

"At Vassar. I know."

Wow. He really had read, and paid attention to, whatever background information he'd been given on her. "So you can guess what this means to me."

"What it means is that I don't have to worry about you donning a wig and climbing out the window to go clubbing."

"I didn't bring my wig." She still clutched the tickets in her hand. "I've left my clubbing days behind."

The look Rafe cast her told her clearly he didn't believe her.

"I'm going to be a model of respectability."

His gaze swept her from head to toe. And though she knew there was no fault he could find with what she wore—it was all designed for the image she needed to project, elegant and stylish—still she sensed something close to disapproval in his frowning assessment.

"So, you didn't even bring the shimmery little dress from the other night?"

"I left it behind with instructions for it to be taken to a charity shop."

"Pity."

"Are you absolutely determined to bait me?" She knew he didn't like the dress; he'd as good as told her. "If you want an argument, just say so. I'll happily give you one." She was still smiling, content and looking forward to the Shakespeare, but she meant what she said.

Something in the vehemence of her response actually seemed to please him. "Just get ready to go out, Precious. We're leaving in fifteen minutes."

As the actors took their final bow after a stunning performance of *A Midsummer Night's Dream*, a tale of love most definitely not running smoothly, Lexie sat back and sighed with pure pleasure.

She glanced at Rafe beside her in their private box. He turned to her, affecting bored indifference. She wasn't going to let him diminish her enjoyment. "That was wonderful. Amazing. Fantastic."

"Rapturous?"

"Yes."

"I'm glad you enjoyed it," he said.

"You enjoyed it, too, didn't you?" She was fairly sure the distant superiority was an act.

"Of course."

"You were laughing." She'd heard him several times throughout the performance. He had a laugh so low and deep and rich it seemed at times to wrap itself around her.

"I said I enjoyed it."

"Then what's with the grumpy act? Did you see one of your girlfriends in the audience, out with another man?"

"No. Let's just go." He stood.

Lexie was loath to leave. "Wasn't Puck fabulous? And this theater…" She looked round the wooden, open-roofed facility, a replica of the one used in Shakespeare's time that had burned down when a prop cannon misfired.

"Save it for Adam," he said, not unkindly. "He's the Shakespeare buff."

"I know. It's just one of the things we have in common."

He rolled his eyes in a most unprincely gesture. "Are you ready yet?" He held out his hand.

"It was really sweet of you to bring me here tonight, when you don't love it."

"Sweet?"

"Yes." He clearly wasn't used to being called sweet, and clearly didn't like it. She took the hand he was still holding out for her, felt his strong fingers fold around hers and, still floating from the performance, stood.

He'd averted his face, was in fact studying the audience as though there was something or someone of the utmost importance out there. He needed to loosen up. Not something she'd ever thought she'd think about Rafe. Whether he'd enjoyed the performance or not, she'd been enraptured, and she was more grateful than he could know that he'd brought her here. On impulse, Lexie leaned forward to kiss his cheek.

At that moment he turned.

For a second, maybe two or three, her lips touched his, warm and soft. And for that sublime second, or two, or three, that simplest of kisses consumed her. Stopped the world around her, stilled everything within her, and then threatened to buckle her knees as heat shot through her.

The rapture of the play was nothing compared to this.

Strong fingers wrapped around her upper arms and set her away from him.

Lifting her hands to her lips, she met his gaze, saw the mirror of her own shock in his darkened eyes. "I'm *so* sorry." She stepped back. "That was not what I meant to happen. I was aiming for your cheek." Lexie pointed at the cheek in question, as though to reinforce her statement. And still he said nothing, didn't laugh or brush off the incident. Surely he realized it *was* unintentional. "You turned." It hadn't even been entirely her fault. Beneath his unflinching scrutiny she faltered. "It was an accident. I've said I'm sorry." He didn't so much as blink. "Say something. Please."

He opened his mouth. It was several seconds before

the words came out. "I guess we're even. Let's go." He pushed aside the curtain behind them and held open the door.

Ten minutes later in the car, as their driver negotiated the London streets, Lexie stared through the window. She'd give anything for the kiss not to have happened. To not have the fact that it did happen hanging between them. Besides, it was a nothing kiss, chaste, and as she'd pointed out, accidental. He couldn't know of the strange heat it had ignited. The heat that had flared further when he'd wrapped his fingers around her arms, when for an instant she had seen fire in his eyes. Fire that she realized now was anger.

Rafe had scarcely spoken since they'd left the theater. They were nearly back at the apartments, and she didn't want the strained silence to go on any longer. He sat leaning back against the seat, as far from her as the confines of the Bentley allowed, head tipped back on the soft leather, eyes closed. But she knew he wasn't sleeping.

Lexie pivoted in her seat to face him. "We're not even."

The eyes opened halfway, the head turned slowly toward her. From beneath his hooded lids, he studied her.

"When you said we were even, were you referring to the time you kissed me at the masquerade ball?"

His response was the barest nod.

"Then I have to disagree."

The angle of his head changed. His eyes widened ever so slightly. It was enough of a reaction that she interpreted it as curiosity, or at least tacit permission to continue.

"There was no tongue in mine." His kiss had been shockingly erotic, igniting her strange, forbidden desires. She sat back in her seat.

There was a moment of surprise, and then the deep rumble of his laughter rolled through the interior of the vehicle, pleasing her inordinately. "Only because I knew who I was kissing this time."

Five

Despite telling herself to forget about it, Lexie was still troubled by that kiss as the royal jet cruised over Europe. Twice now she and Rafe had kissed. Both times accidentally. And both times, for no good reason, their kiss had left her tossing through the night, tormented by darkly erotic dreams. Dreams that took the kiss as a starting point.

Her only consolation was that if a kiss from Rafe, a man she mostly didn't like, could have that effect on her, kissing Adam was going to be knee-weakeningly devastating.

Fortunately, once they got off this plane she'd have little more to do with Rafe and the provocation of his presence. But for now, he sat a short way away from her, stretched out on a sumptuous cream leather couch and seemingly engrossed in a book. One he'd opened immediately after seating himself. The book was, she suspected, his way of avoiding her. But it also gave her leave to study him. His sentiments showed clearly as he read, occasionally frowning, sometimes almost smiling. Though she wouldn't allow herself to look properly at his lips.

He read fast, turning the pages rapidly, his deft fingers ready in anticipation of the next page moments after turning the last. He had nice hands. Was she allowed to think that about Adam's brother?

He glanced up and caught her watching him.

"Good book?" she asked, trying to cover the fact that she'd been staring.

"Yes." He tilted it up so she could see the cover of the political thriller before returning his attention back to it, clearly shutting her out.

That was a good thing. They didn't need to be chatting. Still, Lexie had to make herself look away from him. Had to stop wondering what really went on inside his head.

She'd tried reading, too, first a book and then a glossy magazine, but she couldn't even concentrate on that. She was too anxious, and it wasn't, she told herself, just because of the inadvertent kiss, because soon that memory would fade. It had to. It was in the past.

And it wasn't because of the irrelevant question prompted by his retort in the limo—that the kiss had gone no further because he'd known who he was kissing. Did that mean he didn't find her attractive? Or that he did, but knew he shouldn't?

Neither answer would be ideal.

Turning away from Rafe, she looked out her window. What ought to concern her now was the future. Her future. She should be thinking about Adam, whom she was about to meet again. Not as an eighteen-year-old, and not through the medium of e-mail, but as a woman, and in person. She was about to truly begin the next phase of her life.

A stunningly beautiful hostess removed the remnants of their lunch from the coffee table between them and informed them they were beginning their descent. Lexie only half heard her.

It remained to be seen whether she ended up staying, falling the rest of the way in love from the halfway state she'd been in for almost as long as she could remember. And convincing Adam to fall in love with her, and eventually, or maybe even soon, marry her, was another thing entirely.

But whatever happened, she'd left her old self and her old life behind.

"You'll see San Philippe to the east in a few minutes."

Rafe's voice startled her. She'd been staring out the window, but she'd scarcely been taking anything in. Far below, the cities and mountains of Europe spread out. Features of the landscape became clearer.

"You can usually catch a glimpse of the palace, as well," he said a few minutes later.

"I see it." She felt excitement rising as the jet lowered and she glimpsed distant turrets.

She would be seeing Adam again soon. She could stop thinking about Rafe.

Miniature horses dotted a field below. "Will Adam be playing polo in the cup match next weekend? Or is his rotator cuff still bothering him?" She was eager to see Adam again, but had to admit she was a little apprehensive, too.

Rafe lifted an eyebrow in enquiry. "You know about his shoulder injury?"

She shrugged. "Ten years is a long while to have… an interest in someone." She wasn't going to say the word *crush,* because it sounded so immature, but that's admittedly what her relationship—again, probably the wrong word—had started out as. "A girl can do a lot of research in that time. I can give you the whole history of it."

"Ever heard of *stalking?*"

He said the word with a bored smile, but Lexie bristled. "It's not like that." At least not anymore. She'd long ago thrown out the embarrassing scrapbook she'd kept as a young teenager, filled with photos of Adam playing polo or attending functions. "I've looked at the odd Web site." No need to give Rafe numbers. But because he was one of the world's most eligible bachelors, plenty of sites followed Adam. "And I've studied the history of San Philippe because it's part of my heritage." And because it was potentially part of her future. "I like to think of it as being well-informed."

"Uh-huh." How did he make those two syllables sound so condescending?

"We have mutual acquaintances, as well."

"Don't feel you have to justify yourself to me."

"I'm not justifying myself, I just think you should be clear on where I stand."

"I think I'm clear." He returned his attention to his book, trying to dismiss her.

She wasn't that easy to dismiss. "And I don't think you are."

He sighed and flipped over a page.

"I'm not obsessive about Adam." He should know that. "I've dated other men. I even imagined myself in love once."

That snagged his attention. He looked back at her. "And?"

She shrugged. "It didn't work out. And not because of anything to do with Adam," she added quickly. Well, not directly, although it was possible that Paul had suffered in comparison. "I've grown and matured, and become my own woman."

"I'm sure you have."

Lexie could think of no witty or even sarcastic retort so she tried for a disdainful look before turning to her window to watch her destiny draw closer, savoring the sense of anticipation as the wheels lowered into position for landing. Rafe didn't understand. She was her own woman and knew her own mind. She just hoped—and had, in fact, planned—that she was the type of woman who appealed to Adam. And his father. Because she'd have to have Prince Henri's blessing. And probably also the approval of palace advisers. And even the public of San Philippe. Which was what was sending her heart into overdrive. Despite her mother's assurances and training, she didn't know if she was cut out for that much scrutiny, for the prospect of such a public failure. What if this was a colossal mistake?

No. Time to stop the negative self-talk. She could do this.

"Talking to yourself?" She looked across to see Rafe watching her, a smile tugging at his lips.

Had she been? "No, of course not." Against her will that smile drew her own out, making it impossible to stay mad at him. "Maybe. I've just realized what a very public spectacle I could make of myself here."

"The palace will be working to keep everything low-key. It won't be too public."

"But still a spectacle?"

"That part's up to you."

The plane touched down, decelerating rapidly. She looked out the window at a waving crowd standing behind a cordoned-off area. "So that crowd out there is normal?"

"There are always a few people with nothing better to do than hang out at the airport when the royal jet flies in."

"That many?"

He followed her gaze and she saw a flash of surprise in his eyes, but he leaned back in his seat. "Give or take a few."

"Wow."

"Don't overthink things."

"What do you mean?" She thought she knew, but talking to him, listening to his deep, calm voice, his soft accent, helped distract her.

"Worrying ahead of time about what people will think or what might go wrong. You'll step off this plane, see Adam and take it from there. One moment at a time."

"Of course we'll be taking things slowly, but controlling my thoughts and anxiety is easier said than done."

"No. It's exactly as easy to say as it is to do. In fact, your thoughts are one of the few things in life you do have control over. And thinking things over and over and round and round in your head, things you can't possibly have any control over—that's not easy. It's also a hell of a waste of mental energy."

"You could be right. But I don't think you really understand."

"I know I'm right." He pulled a business card from his pocket, flipped it over and wrote on the back before handing it to her.

She looked at the cell phone number scrawled elegantly across the card.

"I may not see that much of you around the palace. That's my private number," he said on a sigh. "In case."

"In case what?"

"In case you don't know which fork to use. I don't know. Just in case. Only a couple of people have it, so if you call, I'll answer it."

"Thank you." It struck her then that with their time in Massachusetts, London and on the plane she'd now spent more consecutive time in Rafe's company than she ever had in Adam's.

"Abuse it and I'll change the number."

Lexie smiled and lapsed into silence. She looked away from the window and at the hands clasped in her lap. After agonizing over what to wear, she'd settled on a skirt and short, tailored jacket. But maybe she should have worn the shift dress. It was probably hot out there. She glanced at Rafe. He wore an open-necked white linen shirt and cream-colored pants. He looked fantastic, as if he'd just stepped off a yacht in the Mediterranean. She chewed her bottom lip.

He sighed. "What are you worried about now?"

She hadn't thought he'd been aware of her. She swallowed. "Would calling you to ask a really stupid question be considered abusing the privilege?"

"A really stupid question like what?"

"Like, do I look okay?"

His gaze swept over her. "Fine."

"What's wrong with it?"

"I said it was fine."

"I know. So what's wrong with it?"

He shook his head. "Nothing. Adam will love it. You look very…regal. Quite proper. The pearls are a great touch."

"But you don't like it?"

He lifted a shoulder. "I'm shallower than Adam. The regal look's not my thing. Give me a short, shimmery black dress anyday."

She smiled. "I hope someday you find a tramp who'll make you very happy."

He smiled back. Finally. His first real smile of the day. A smile a person could almost grow to depend upon, bringing with it a little jolt to her insides, stronger even than that first cup of coffee in the morning. "I intend to search the world over till I find her."

Stairs were wheeled to the jet and the crew opened the door.

"Right, then, Alexia, let's get this show on the road."

Rafe stood, ready to walk with her to the exit and thank the pilot and crew who stood waiting by the door. Ready to hand her over to Adam and put her from his mind. She slipped his card into her purse and stood, too. Glancing at the door, then back at him, she placed a tentative hand on his arm. "Will you call me Lexie?"

He hesitated.

"I need one person here who does."

He nodded. Reluctantly. "Lexie," he sighed her name. Her grateful smile was pure innocence, and all he could think was sexy, sexy, Lexie. What he'd like to say to her and do with her were eons away from innocence. It had been torment enough just sitting so close beside her in the theater last night. Her rapturous sighs, her delighted laughter. And then that kiss. Damn that stupid kiss, that taste of temptation, that taste of the forbidden. He hadn't been joking when he'd said the only reason there was no tongue in it was because he knew who she was. That was also the only reason he hadn't kept her in that box and gone on kissing her. They wouldn't have been disturbed. He could have slid his hands up her legs, pulled her against him. He could have— *Stop.* He had to stop this. He'd call the sophisticated and available divorcée he'd met last week as soon as he handed Lexie—Alexia, dammit—over.

There would be two cars at the airport. He and Adam seldom traveled together. It wouldn't do to have both male heirs wiped out at once in the event of either an accident or an act of terrorism. He'd be on his own at last. Away from her smile, away from her scent. Away from her hopeful, idealistic naivety.

He'd hand her to Adam, he'd see the two of them together and cement it in his mind that she belonged with his brother, her knight in shining armor. The most she could ever be to him was his sister-in-law.

Security staff escorted them to the terminal. Alexia walked close to him. There was tension in the rigid set to her shoulders, in the stiffly held neck. He wanted to take her hand, in a brotherly fashion, he tried to tell himself. Reassuring. But far too open to misinterpretation. So instead he turned to Joseph, the family's head of security. "This is quite a crowd." Because despite what he'd said to Alexia, the crowd was considerably larger than he'd expected.

"The forthcoming anniversary celebrations. There's been something of an upsurge of interest in all things royal. It's been building for some time."

Had it? He hadn't noticed.

"And of course there's the young lady herself."

She didn't turn her head, but Rafe knew she'd heard. She really would make a good royal. He asked on her behalf. "Alexia? Why?"

"The people know she's a Wyndham. They know the families are close. There's been some speculation."

Speculation that because her family once had a claim to the throne that a union now between the two families would somehow complete a circle.

Lexie did glance at him then, her face a little paler than before. He winked. "Just smile and wave, babe. Smile and wave."

She winked back, a twinkle in her moss-green eyes, then did exactly as he'd suggested. A cheer went up in the crowd along with hundreds of fluttering San Philippe flags.

Minutes later, Rafe leaned against a pillar and watched her from across the royal lounge in the terminal building. Prince Henri, looking far too pleased with himself, had formally welcomed her. Rafe had been surprised to see his father here, revealing just how much importance he was placing on this venture succeeding. Then his sister, Rebecca, had hugged her, and last but by no means least, she had turned to Adam.

And now Lexie—no, Alexia—stood talking to his older brother, pleasure shining in her face.

Adam smiled back at her, his charismatic best. Rafe could discern none of the resentment he would have felt if he was meeting a woman he'd been told he was going to marry.

Of course, Adam was better than that. He was both diplomatic and charming. It was easy to see why Alexia, Alexia, Alexia—he'd say it over to himself a hundred times if he had to—fancied herself half in love with him. He just hoped Adam valued what he was getting. Because though he could be diplomatic and charming— that was part of his job description—he could also be

self-absorbed, distant and, well, boring. And though
Rafe had originally thought Alexia boring, too, he'd
realized the conservatism was a front. A charade, even
if she believed it, for the role she wanted to play.

Rafe watched as Adam touched her arm and smiled.
Alexia laughed. Demurely.

Mission accomplished. He was free to forget about
her and get on with his own life. Rafe turned and slipped
away.

Six

Lexie tried to concentrate. Her dinner companion, a senior San Philippe politician, his chest weighted down with medals, whose name she had already forgotten, was explaining the evolution of the country's political system. Sadly, the throbbing in her head and the complexities of the system combined to leave her floundering. The enthusiastic playing of the band wasn't helping her efforts. She could only hope that her smiles and nods at least convinced her companion that she was both following and interested in his discourse, and not secretly wondering whether it was too soon to leave. He paused to reach across the table for a profiterole.

At first the state dinner had been exciting, the long tables set with so much silver cutlery and crystal that beneath the light of the chandeliers they gleamed with the brilliance of diamonds. Then there were the guests, the elite and powerful of San Philippe, the beautiful of San Philippe. But after a while it had become just another dinner spent having to make conversation with people she didn't know.

Which wouldn't have been so bad if it hadn't been for her steadily worsening headache. A maid had styled her hair. Lexie loved the elegant twist—it was perfect for a formal dinner, but she hadn't realized quite how tightly her hair had been pulled until the aching in her head began.

She found herself yearning for pizza eaten in silence while she looked out over city lights at nighttime, her feet resting on an ottoman.

Massaging her temple, Lexie looked at the head table, where Adam sat deep in conversation with an elder statesman. He had explained that it would be best for them not to be seated together tonight. No point in adding fire to the already circulating rumors just yet. She completely understood and agreed. Already she felt as if she were under a microscope.

Looking around she caught sight of Rafe, farther up her table and on the opposite side, watching her. She couldn't fathom the expression in his dark eyes and couldn't quite explain the effect it had on her, causing a strange discomfort. He raised his wineglass in a mock salute, then turned to the voluptuous, sophisticated blonde at his side.

Lexie's companion finished his profiterole, wiped cream from his fingers onto his linen napkin and invited her to dance. As far as she could see, she had no choice but to accept. Taking her arm, he escorted her to the dance floor and pulled her into a formal and rigid clasp for the waltz. Lexie looked over his shoulder to avoid staring at the droplet of cream caught in his moustache.

As they danced, he continued talking politics. Specifically, his rise through parliament, and the problems with the younger politicians who thought they knew everything. Who knew one song could last so long?

Finally, the music slowed and quieted, but then segued immediately into another melody. "By the time I was elected for my third term," he said, giving her no opportunity to decline another dance.

Rafe appeared behind his shoulder and tapped it. "Mind if I cut in, Humphrey?"

Humphrey, that was his name.

Humphrey released her, took a step back, bowed slightly, then bowed again to Rafe. "Of course not, sir." He moved aside.

Rafe stepped in front of her. His gaze swept the length of her beaded, ice-blue gown; his undisguised masculine approval warmed her. Gentle yet sure, he took her hand in his, placed his other hand at the curve of her waist. "Thank you," she said, when what she really wanted to do was hug him in sheer gratitude.

"Dancing with Humphrey after being seated next to him for the last two hours seemed a little too much to have to put up with. Even for a woman who wants to marry Adam."

"That almost sounds chivalrous. And definitely thoughtful."

"Hmm. I suppose it was," he said, sounding surprised. They danced a few steps. "Ironic, really, isn't it?"

"What is?" She rested her left hand on the broad strength of his shoulder, felt the power beneath her touch.

"That tonight you really do have a headache," he said as they began to waltz, "but don't feel you can leave."

She hadn't thought she'd given it away, or that Rafe had been watching her closely enough to notice. "My penance, I guess. Though I have to admit I was wondering about the protocol for leaving."

He grinned and said nothing further. They danced in silence, his movements altogether more fluid and easy than Humphrey's as he led her around the room. When the band next stopped, he dropped his hand from her waist and shifted to stand beside her, keeping her right hand held in his. "This way," he said. They were on the far side of the dance floor and he began leading her, not back to her seat, but in the opposite direction.

"Where are we going?"

"You want to leave, don't you?"

She hesitated. "I shouldn't."

He led her onward. "Why not? You've had a long day, and you're jet-lagged."

"Same as you."

"Which is why I'm leaving."

"Really?"

He stopped and turned to face her. "There are some

things I don't joke about. Besides, you have a headache. A real one this time."

Leave her first official dinner early? Wouldn't that be bad form? "You said yourself that I'd have to sit through these things till the bitter end."

"You will have to stay. Once you become princess."

"If."

"If. Whatever. But now? Now you have a valid excuse. Now you're under the radar, just. Now might be your only chance."

She glanced at the head table.

"Adam won't mind." He read her thoughts, and mercifully didn't add that Adam likely wouldn't notice. They'd had a lovely but brief meeting this afternoon. He had shown her round some of the palace's enormous manicured gardens, including the renowned labyrinth.

As they'd walked arm in arm in the sunshine, he had explained the gardeners' efforts at conservation of his country's native flora. He was knowledgeable and gentlemanly, and alert to her fatigue. It had been a relief to be in the company of someone easy to be with, not like Rafe, who always seemed to be watching her and whose presence filled Lexie with a strange tension.

She and Adam had parted to prepare for this evening. But throughout the meal, he had only once looked her way and had nodded—almost paternally—at her before returning to his conversation.

Rafe, on the other hand, had caught her out more than once looking at him.

"He asked me to keep an eye on you."

She smiled. "What did you say?" She couldn't imagine he would have been pleased to have his babysitting duties extended.

"I said yes."

"Just yes?"

He smiled back, real warmth in his eyes. "Of course, just yes."

"Liar."

His smile widened. "Come on, Lexie."

Escaping with Rafe held infinitely more appeal than staying. But it was his use of her name that swayed her. Reminded her that he was her friend. Because only her friends called her Lexie.

None of the staff seemed surprised to see them as they slipped through a kitchen the size of a house. She couldn't suppress a gurgle of laughter as Rafe grasped her hand to lead her around counters and past the sous-chefs and kitchen hands, most of whom seemed to be shouting at each other.

"Rupert." Rafe acknowledged the man who stood, arms folded, surveying the entire kitchen.

Rupert, impressive gray sideburns showing from beneath his chef's hat, glanced at his watch. "You lasted well tonight, sir."

"By the time I'm your age, I expect I'll be able to last a whole evening."

"I'm sure everyone looks forward to that day."

"Everyone except me," Rafe said on a smile, not breaking his stride.

"I take it you do this often?" Lexie asked.

"Since the very first state dinner I attended. Rupert

was on dishes back then. He helped me find my way out of this maze."

"Couldn't we just have gone out the doors we came in?"

"Far less attention drawn to us this way. Too many people watch the doors."

"It's only because of my headache that I'm leaving. I have a valid reason. I don't need to be sneaking about." Although, oddly, from the moment she'd decided to leave, the headache had begun to diminish.

"So if I told you about a nightclub not too far away, where they play the most amazing music?"

"I wouldn't be even remotely tempted." Though she couldn't help but wonder what it would be like to dance with Rafe. Truly dance. And to watch the way he moved. Not like their earlier formal waltz, which she now recognized as merely a part of his escape plan.

They passed through another door and stepped into an empty, dimly lit corridor. As the door swung shut behind them, the chaos and noise of the kitchen ceased. Silence swamped them. He stopped and turned to face her, blocking her way. "Liar," he said in a whisper. "You'd be tempted."

And suddenly she wasn't sure what temptation he was referring to. The temptation of dancing or the temptation of him? The memory of the kiss that shouldn't have happened came back to her, flooding her with warmth. And she remembered, too, the even earlier kiss. One that back then had hinted at things she'd only guessed at.

Lexie couldn't speak, couldn't move.

Abruptly Rafe stepped back and turned to keep walking. Lexie clenched her fists at her side. She just needed to get away from here, away from him. She needed to spend time with Adam.

They continued in silence, along corridors, past opulent room after opulent room, climbed broad, sweeping staircases, till finally he stopped in front of a door she recognized as her own.

Lexie pushed open the door and turned back to face Rafe, keeping one hand on the handle. "Thank you."

He was looking over her shoulder and she followed his gaze, saw her nightgown, green and flimsy, laid out on her turned-back bed. Then she looked in the region of Rafe's too-broad chest. "Good night."

Gentle fingers under her chin tipped her head up so that short of closing her eyes she had to meet his gaze. She couldn't interpret what she saw in his dark eyes. It was close to anger, and yet not. "Good night, Lexie." He stood close, radiating heat.

For a second neither of them moved. She felt as powerless as she had outside the kitchen, as though he somehow sapped her strength, diverted her will. In a way that was all wrong and exhilaratingly right.

All wrong. She focused on that thought. She was here to get to know Adam, not the Frog Prince. She wanted Adam to look at her with something of what was in Rafe's gaze. She wanted to feel with Adam that same yearning she felt now to lean into Rafe, to slide her arms around him.

She was lonely. That's all it was. She was away from her home, her country, and despite her years of contact with Adam, the last few days with Rafe meant it was him she knew best. It was only natural that she wanted to turn to him. Once she'd spent more time with Adam, that would change.

Her breath caught as Rafe lifted his hand to her hair. She felt quick deft movements and then her hair tumbled down around her shoulders. "Better," he murmured, and she wasn't sure whether it was a statement or a question. He ran his fingers down a lock, then lifted her hand, turned it over, uncurled her fist and dropped her clips into her palm.

"Go to bed, Lexie."

Rafe tried to concentrate on his father's words as the prince made his speech for the official opening of the anniversary-week celebrations. The proximity of the woman seated on his left between him and his brother made the task almost impossible. The woman who'd been nothing but trouble since that first day in Boston. Big trouble—no matter how placid and regal she looked in her rose-colored dress with her beautiful hair pulled up into a twist at the back of her head.

When he'd convinced her that coming here was the right thing to do, he'd thought that that would be his reprieve. Showed how wrong he was.

At least now she wasn't his problem. Her relationship with Adam was progressing. They'd spent most of the two days she'd been here together. The fact that she was seated at Adam's right was significant. Did she know that little tidbit, and what it signaled, would have the royal-watchers all aflutter and would be all over the newspapers by tomorrow morning?

She was getting her wish, her dream come true.

He'd been observing—watching and listening to Adam. His brother was solicitous toward Lexie, charming. Smiling and handsome. They looked good together. They made the perfect couple. That fact should please Rafe.

But it didn't.

He didn't know why he was so fascinated with Lexie. Possibly it was only because he couldn't have her. Couldn't *ever* have her. Maybe he needed to date even more. Find someone like her. No. Not like her. Because he didn't want serious. The problem with Lexie was that she confused him, somehow tied him up in knots, made him forget the principles that let him comfortably live his life.

Suddenly she laughed, along with the crowd, at one of his father's jokes, the sound a delight.

As soon as the speeches were done—there would be several more after this one—he was getting out of here. He needed to be somewhere, anywhere else. Maybe even a different country, if he could arrange it.

Lexie glanced at him, her face alight with her recent laughter, her eyes sparkling.

She leaned closer and started to speak.

"Lexie, listen to my father." He cut off whatever she'd been about to say.

Lush, rose-colored lips shut together.

He hadn't done it to stop her talking, although that was probably a good thing, but he'd realized his father had started telling a story about Marie, Rafe's mother, something he'd seldom done in the years since her death, preferring to keep his memories private. And he was discussing his hopes and dreams, something he never did, either, because he didn't believe in them, believing in facts and work and duty.

Henri turned to the side of the dais and Lexie's mother, Antonia, walked in, looking both serene and smug as she made her way to stand beside Rafe's father.

They both looked at Adam and Lexie. It meant only one thing. Rafe followed their gazes, saw Lexie's surprise and confusion. Adam wasn't confused, Adam knew precisely what was happening, though Rafe was guessing Adam hadn't sanctioned it because he saw the infinitesimal shake of Adam's head, the subtle glare at their father.

"We are so pleased," his father said, "to announce tonight that we have each given our permission for my son and Alexia Wyndham Jones to become engaged. And our blessing to the future joining of the Wyndham and Marconi families."

The crowd erupted in a joyous roar. Beside Rafe, Lexie gasped and stiffened. Adam grasped her hand. The gesture looked affectionate, but Rafe suspected that his brother was also keeping her in her seat, because she looked ready to flee. Over the rousing applause, he couldn't hear what Adam whispered to a suddenly pale Lexie. Flashlights burst in a prolonged bright explosion.

Just days ago on the plane Lexie had told him that

she and his brother were going to take things slowly and quietly. And he'd told her the palace would be working to keep things low-key. Clearly he'd forgotten to factor his father's desire for a royal wedding into the equation.

Good old Dad. The family motto should be changed from Honor and Valor to Make It Happen—However You Can.

As the applause died away and his father finished speaking, Rafe leaned in to Lexie, his soon-to-be sister-in-law. "Congratulations."

She turned, and for a second he saw a plea in her wide eyes. Then it was gone and she smiled, a polite, brittle smile. "Thank you."

"Didn't know this was coming?"

She kept that smile fixed in place. "I'll admit it's something of a surprise." The smile wobbled a little. "I don't… I'm not…"

She couldn't look for support from him. "You must be thrilled. You've got your wish, your happily-ever-after."

The smile firmed. "Yes. Yes, I have. But your father only said he's given his permission. We're not actually engaged."

Yet. Clearly she didn't have a complete grasp on how things worked in his father's world. Adam may not have slipped a ring on her finger, but that part was now merely a formality. His gaze dropped to her temporarily unadorned fingers where they lay curled white-knuckled in her lap. "You should unclench your hands."

Adam stood to speak and walked to the lectern to the sound of rapturous applause. "Did Adam know about Dad's permission being granted and announced tonight?" Rafe asked. Because Adam, if unchecked, could be a little like their father. Once he'd committed to a course of action he had a way of making people fall in with him. Rafe didn't want to have to intervene.

"Apparently, your father raised it as a possibility yesterday. But he'd said he didn't think it was a good idea. That we weren't ready."

"Dad being ready and the timing being right are the only things that matter."

"Anyway, it'll be easier now. Adam and I can legitimately spend more time together. I can accompany him publicly." She'd tensed up again, her shoulders rigid, as she repeated what sounded like his brother's words.

"I wish you all the best."

"Thank you." Her hands clenched back into fists.

"You do make a nice couple."

"I know."

"The photos of the two of you at the orchestra were very fetching."

"Adam says that's largely why your father announced it. The photos, the speculation."

Unfortunately, that announcement now meant that Rafe couldn't leave the country as he'd planned. His leaving might be misinterpreted, or worse, might be correctly interpreted. "Dad has the very best PR advisers guiding him," he said. "Not to mention a will of steel. He's also shrewd and wily. And he most definitely likes to stay a step ahead of the press. They have kind of a love-hate relationship. He's misled them more than once, and though they resent it, they respect him for it, too."

She smiled. "I like him. Your father."

"By and large, so do I."

She blinked her surprise.

"He also has some unlikable qualities, but we usually ignore those." His father was grinning broadly at Lexie from his seat behind the lectern. "He likes you, too. He always has. But that doesn't mean he won't use you to suit his own purposes. In the nicest possible way."

"To suit his purposes? What does it matter to him if Adam and I get engaged or not?"

Rafe felt a sudden, cold stillness within him. She didn't know. No one had told her that Adam had more or less been instructed to marry her. And rather more than less. Rafe certainly wasn't the one to break that news to her, at least not here and not now. That was a job for someone far more tactful than he. Someone who loved her and could convince her of that.

Lexie was silent for a few steps. "Anyway, I'm used to dealing with people who like to get their own way," she glanced at her mother. "And I'm not quite the pushover I seem."

"Good for you."

The hunted look left her eyes to be replaced by the strength he'd seen in the States. "This won't happen unless I'm certain it's what I want."

Good. That meant he didn't have to worry about protecting anyone from anyone. Not Adam from Lexie or Lexie from Adam. Apparently, they both knew what they wanted and how to get it.

Two mornings later, Lexie slipped through the hushed corridors of the palace. This early in the morning there was little activity, only the occasional servant walking quietly but purposefully. Other than a respectful nod, they paid her no attention, showed no reaction to her attire. The palace was old, its layout confusing, but despite a few wrong turns she made it to the basement level and the door to the private gymnasium. She needed to work off some of the confusion and uncertainty that plagued her. She'd told Rafe the engagement wouldn't happen unless she was certain it was what she wanted. The trouble was, she still wasn't certain. Adam was lovely, everything she knew him to be, and she really liked him, but…she had too many buts.

She also needed to shut out, for a time, awareness of the building public expectation. Already this morning's papers were filled with photos of her and Adam. Some commentators were even discussing possible wedding dates.

A wave of rock music hit her as she pushed open the door and stepped inside.

Only one other person was in here, long muscular legs striding powerfully on a treadmill. He glanced over his shoulder as she came in, and if he hadn't seen her she would have backed quickly out. But Rafe, the man she wanted to stop thinking about, had already punched the buttons to slow his pace. She hadn't seen him yesterday, and had been secretly glad of the reprieve. He wiped his face with a small towel, then lowered the volume on the music. "Morning."

"Morning." The word came out far too husky, on account of being the first word she'd spoken since getting up not long ago. She hung her sweatshirt from a hook next to the much bigger sweatshirt already there and turned.

He smiled. A flash of white, perfect teeth. A gleam of knowledge and amusement in his eyes. "Running, rowing, weights or stairs? Though hardly anyone ever uses the stairs. There are enough of them throughout the palace." He ran easily as he spoke, arms swinging at his sides. His gaze slid over her, took in her hair tied back into a high ponytail, dropped to her racer-back top, lowered to her Lycra shorts and her legs, which were bare except for her trainers.

Her insides tightened and heated. She cleared her throat. "Running." That was what she'd sought out the gym for. She'd wanted to be alone with her thoughts, and running usually helped her clarify things. Already she knew that Rafe's presence would make that all but impossible because he was at least half the reason her thoughts needed clarifying in the first place. Him and the reactions he stirred, sometimes irritation, sometimes companionship, but more often than not longing and desire. Those last two were not what she wanted to feel for him. She wanted to feel them for Adam. And yet when she'd had dinner with Adam last night, she'd felt... friendship and companionship. Important qualities—a good foundation. But she wanted more and didn't know whether that was unreasonable, or just too soon.

Lexie crossed to the second treadmill, a few feet from Rafe, stood on its platform and considered the array of buttons and readouts in front of her that looked like they belonged on the Starship *Enterprise*.

"Bridge to McCoy?" Rafe got off his treadmill.

She grinned. "Exactly what I was thinking." And exactly the sort of thought—so in tune with hers—that added to her confusion.

He stepped onto the stationary edge of her treadmill. "What do you want? Tell me."

Oh, boy, there was a loaded question, when this vision of masculinity stood so close, radiating heat, his tanned skin glistening with the sheen of sweat. He'd brought his water bottle over with him and tipped it to his mouth. Lexie watched the slide of his Adam's apple as he swallowed. "I like to start off slow."

He flicked her a glance that tripped her train of thought. The glance returned, his gaze held hers, a laughing question in his dark eyes, but something else, too, something deep, something light years away from amusement.

No way could she now say, *and to build to harder and faster,* which in her naivety had been the rest of her intended sentence. She cleared her throat, hoped he wouldn't notice the heat building in her face. "I thought I'd do about forty minutes, with a few hills."

He reached past her, his chest close to her shoulder, pushed a few buttons and her treadmill began to move, slowly at first, its speed gradually increasing. Her walk morphed into a jog. And still Rafe stood there. Close. Managing to smell enticing, masculine. "You're up early."

"So are you."

"Sleep well?" he asked.

"Yes," she lied. She didn't tell him of her dreams.

"It can take a while to adjust to the time difference,"

he said, apparently seeing through her lie if not the reason for it.

Rafe stepped away, then came back a few seconds later to deposit a bottle of chilled water in her bottle holder.

"Thanks."

He returned to his treadmill, brought it back up to speed. "How was dinner last night?"

"Amazing."

"Adam took you up the San Philippe tower?"

"Yes. The view over the city at night was incredible." They'd had an entire level of the revolving restaurant to themselves. "And the food was divine." The evening had been really…nice. Adam had been a little tired, and so had she. But she at least had managed to stay awake during the ride back to the palace.

Rafe pressed a button on his treadmill and ran faster. "So, the engagement's going well? Adam's living up to your expectations?"

"I like him. He's really…nice." There was that word again.

Rafe shot her a look. "Damned with faint praise."

"It wasn't faint praise. Just because no one's ever called you nice."

"Not the women I've dated, anyway."

She wondered just what they did call him. Charming? Suave? Passionate? Electric? Till it ended, because from what Adam had told her yesterday and last night, Rafe's relationships never lasted long. Things ended before they got to the stage of him bringing anyone home to "meet Dad." "And do they call you the same sorts of things after you've dumped them as they do when you're dating?"

His bark of laughter sounded loud in the gym. "No, they don't. But I'm not always the one doing the dumping."

"No. I understand that sometimes you orchestrate it so that they dump you." His theory apparently being that if he never stayed the night, and never brought a woman to his own bed, his intentions, or lack of them, were obvious. "Or they let go because they realize you really have no intention of settling down, but mostly they never wanted anything serious, either, because that's the type of woman you look for."

"My, you did do your research on the Marconi family."

"And Adam and Rebecca have both talked to me about you. I think they worry about you."

"I think they're jealous of me."

"That wasn't the feeling I got."

He ran a few more seconds before adding, "At least the women I like don't call me *nice*. And I take that omission as a compliment."

"I wouldn't. Because when I said Adam was nice I meant it as a compliment. He's considerate, and he has an understated humor that can be really funny, and we have lots in common."

"I'm thrilled to hear it." Rafe increased the volume of the music, upped his speed again, and without breaking his stride pulled his T-shirt over his head and tossed it onto the floor.

Now seemed like a good time to stop talking, stop glancing at him and focus solely on her running.

They ran in unison, Lexie finally finding her rhythm, channeling her energy into her stride. Droplets of sweat ran down her face, trickled between her breasts. She was sure it wasn't princesslike, scarcely even ladylike. Her mother had a saying about horses sweating, men perspiring, and ladies only glowing. If that was the case, she was glowing fit to light up the whole gymnasium.

At about the same time they slowed their machines to a cool-down jog and then a walk before stopping. They stretched hamstrings and calves in silence. Crossing the floor, she followed Rafe's example, dropping her towel into the wicker hamper.

"What about you, Rafe? You've never fallen in love? Never met anyone you want to settle down with?"

He laughed as he turned to lift their sweatshirts from the hooks by the door. His back and shoulders glistened. His skin would taste salty. Lexie quashed the errant thoughts about the taste of Rafe, about her lips on his skin. Thoughts that had no place in her head.

"That's like asking if I've ever met anyone I want to climb Mount Everest with," he said as he tossed her sweatshirt to her, "when I have no desire to climb Mount Everest in the first place." Finally, he pulled his sweatshirt over his head, covering the too-distracting expanse of masculine skin and muscle.

"Everyone wants to find someone to share their life with." Lexie pushed her arms into the sleeves of her sweatshirt, shrugged it onto her shoulders and turned her attention to the zip.

Rafe's eyes tracked the movement of her zipper as she pulled it up. "Why do so many people assume that?" He turned away and held open the door. "I've met mountaineers who assume everyone, even if only secretly, wants to climb Mount Everest."

She stopped in front of him, not prepared to let him so easily dismiss the conversation. "Imagine the sense of achievement and satisfaction."

"You want to summit Everest?" He studied her face, his own thoughtful and serious.

"Well, no," she admitted, trying to ignore the building heat that had nothing to do with the exertion of her run and everything to do with standing close to Rafe. This was the reaction she wanted when she was with Adam. Hard to achieve when given the opportunity of private time, like last night in the car, he fell asleep. There was nothing sleepy about Rafe: he was vitality and masculinity personified. "But just imagine." She tried to keep her own imaginings on topic. Mount Everest. They were talking about Mount Everest.

"I'd rather not. And ditto for the settling down. I'm a happy man, Lexie. Happier than most men I know. Including the married ones." There was a warning in his words, in his eyes.

"You do have a zest for life. I think it's probably what some women—" if she said "some women" she was clearly exempting herself "—find attractive." She took the steps that carried her past him. "Like the woman with the long black hair?"

Rafe frowned, a good impersonation of incomprehension. But Lexie knew better. She'd seen the two of them with her own eyes.

"I saw you. Yesterday. As Adam and I were going to dinner. He was on the phone and I was looking out the window. He'd wanted to show me the old part of the city." They'd driven over cobbled streets with ornate, gracious old buildings that came right to the street front. "You were standing on the path, and she was there, in an open doorway. She was very beautiful." Lexie had seen that much as the woman had looked smilingly, perhaps adoringly, up at Rafe before stepping aside to let him in.

Rafe's brow cleared. He studied Lexie long enough to make her uncomfortable, a smile tilting one corner of his lips. "Yes, Adelaide is beautiful," he finally said.

"That's it?"

"You want more?"

"No. It's none of my business."

"You're right. It's not. But I'll tell you this much. She's not my Everest. Not even a foothill."

"Does she know that?"

"Of course."

"I didn't mention her to Adam."

He cut her another look, but didn't respond.

Activity in the halls, particularly on the lower levels, had increased from when she'd made her way down. And this time she did draw glances. Although given that the most lingering glances were from the female staff, she was assuming they were lingering on Rafe, not on her. She didn't blame them. Her gaze wanted to linger, too. She kept it focused straight ahead.

Her steps slowed as they reached her corridor. "Apparently, all of your friends are bachelors. And when they find partners and marry, your contact generally dies off."

"Not true," he said at her side. "I have friends who are married. I must have." They stopped outside her door, Rafe silent and thinking. "Mark and Karen," he announced proudly. "They're married, they even have a baby. I'm going to become its godfather at the christening in a few days. Though it has to be said, Mark's not as much fun as he used to be. Which is what happens when people marry. They get caught up in each other. Two's company and what have you."

"Can't you see you're shutting yourself off from even the possibility of happiness?"

"Can't you see that I *am* happy?"

"Adam says you feel uncomfortable around couples. It makes you realize the emptiness of your lifestyle."

Rafe laughed. "Perhaps Adam's transferring his feelings to me, because, Precious, that's not what I feel." They were standing close. "But surely you and Adam had better things to talk about than me?" His words were low and curious and teasing. "Otherwise I'd suggest you and Adam have problems."

She didn't step back, didn't want to reveal how unsettling his proximity was. She lifted her chin. "Don't flatter yourself. Of course we talked about other things. You were one brief snippet in the whole evening." She didn't detail the other topics, affairs of state, diplomatic considerations, the upcoming anniversary celebrations. Sadly, Rafe had for Lexie been the most interesting topic of conversation. She'd tried to draw Adam out about himself, but it wasn't till she'd lain in bed that night thinking over her evening that she realized how skillfully evasive he'd been.

"Today we're going to the Royal Garden Show, and tonight we're attending the orchestra."

"You didn't suggest a nightclub? Some dancing?"

"Do you think he'd like it?" she asked, hopefully. It hadn't occurred to her. She didn't think Adam was the type.

"No. He'd hate it. Pressing crowds, loud music."

"Just like the orchestra?"

He laughed but quickly sobered. "How much of yourself are you willing to sacrifice for him?"

Lexie lifted her chin. "He's not asking me to sacrifice anything."

"Because he doesn't know you. Doesn't know that he's not meeting the real you."

"I have more than one side to my personality. He is meeting the real me. He already knows me better than you ever will."

Rafe raised his eyebrows. "Sure." Not believing her any more than she believed herself. Rafe seemed to see a part of her she didn't even acknowledge she had.

He reached past her, turned the handle of her door and pushed it open. Then he turned her with his hands on her shoulders. His voice was close to her ear, his body close behind her. "Go have a shower, Lexie. Make yourself look regal. Your prince is waiting."

Seven

There were just three of them, and too much food, left at the shady outdoor table. The scent of roses drifted on the breeze. Adam sat with his phone pressed to his ear, and though Lexie wasn't actively listening she couldn't help hearing him patiently placating whoever was on the other end.

They had spent a pleasant afternoon together yesterday. She was slowly getting used to the concept of their engagement, and she certainly felt comfortable with Adam. They talked easily about so many subjects: Shakespeare, gardening, his charities, his work with the government. And when there were silences, they were companionable. They didn't thrum with tension and anticipation. Not like—

She glanced at Rafe, the other person at the table,

leaning back easily in his chair, his meal half-eaten, watching both her and Adam. He'd come late to the lunch. A shaggy gray dog, close to the size of a small horse, lay at his side, its eyes following Rafe's every movement.

"The dog's yours?"

"I've moved on from frogs."

She met his smile, felt the curious warmth it inevitably stirred. "What's his name?"

"Duke."

"What breed?"

"Irish wolfhound."

And there was that silence again. Even with Adam beside her talking, the short distance, the width of a table between her and Rafe was filled with the tension of thoughts and words not spoken. Of mistaken touches. Why did he fascinate her so, and how did she stop it?

He lifted his glass in a silent, almost insolent, toast to her.

"I apologize, Alexia." Adam disconnected his call. "Only half a dozen people have my private number. And they only call if it's important."

He hadn't given the number to her. Not like— She cut off that thought. "It's okay, I understand. There must be incredible demands on your time."

"There are, and there always will be—" he covered her hand with his "—but they're not so important that I wouldn't rather spend my time with a beautiful woman."

He was talking about her? He meant well, but probably had no idea how rehearsed and…insincere he sounded.

Adam turned to his suddenly coughing brother and thumped him lightly on the back. He didn't see the unholy amusement dancing in Rafe's eyes.

Lexie focused on Adam. "Are you still okay for riding the palace grounds this afternoon?"

"Absolutely. I have a couple more phone calls to make first. We'll meet in an hour."

Time together, doing something she loved and that Adam had assured her he, too, enjoyed, would surely be good.

"And tonight, I've planned a dinner. It'll be just the two of us." He smiled, real warmth in his eyes. Eyes that weren't the same dark honey as Rafe's, didn't have the simmering depths or the hint of cynicism or mystery about them, or even that sporadic amusement. But nice eyes.

His phone rang again. He looked at her. "I really am sorry about this, Alexia."

"Please, it's okay. I'll go get changed."

She stood as Adam answered his call. Both men stood, as well, a courtesy she still wasn't used to. Her gaze went to Rafe's, to eyes that saw too much. His gaze was carefully neutral now.

Rafe watched his brother as he finished his third call and turned to him. "No," he said, before Adam could ask.

It didn't stop him. "Take Alexia for the ride through the grounds for me, Rafe? Please."

Rafe dipped a chunk of bread in extra-virgin olive oil, pressed from the palace's olive grove. "Take her yourself."

"I can't. You heard that phone call."

"She could walk the labyrinth." That was a nice, solitary, time-consuming activity.

"She's walked it already."

"Then get Rebecca to take her riding. They get along well. It'll be nice for both of them."

"Rebecca's spending the afternoon with Alexia's mother. Dad's in Paris. You're the only one of us even close to available. It will only take a couple of hours."

"She's here to get to know you, not me."

"We spent all yesterday together." Adam at least had the grace to sound defensive.

"Ah, yes, the inner workings of the museum, dark, dusty corridors. You really know how to show a girl a good time."

"Alexia enjoyed the museum. She has a keen interest in history. Particularly the history of San Philippe."

Alexia. Lexie. Sexy Lexie, whom he'd been doing his best to avoid without being obvious about it. Sexy Lexie, whose hair he wanted to unpin and plunge his fingers into. Whose neck he wanted to kiss. Whose laughter he wanted to hear. Whose lips— Mustn't think about that. The same mantra he'd repeated silently whenever he was in her company and too often even when he wasn't. "Are you sure she enjoyed it? She's polite. She even managed to look interested when Humphrey was haranguing her at the dinner the other night."

"He wasn't, was he?"

"He was. Which you would have known if you'd been paying attention."

"Some of us have other demands on our attention."

Rafe let the implication that he had no demands on his pass. "Which is why you should *make* the time to ride the grounds with her."

"Fine. I will. You take my place as the chair of the meeting on the Global Garden. There's an updated dossier you'll need to read. Martin can brief you, as well. It should only take an hour, two at the most, to bring you up to speed. And the meeting itself, if you keep dissent under control, will be another two. Just be careful to keep a lid firmly on the diplomatic fracas threatening to blow up in our faces. Our so-called ambassador has been treading on toes again."

"Okay, you win. I think I'll put her on Rebecca's gray mare." Martyrdom had only so much to recommend it. Though he knew he was letting himself in for an altogether different kind of torture.

Adam smiled, looking suspiciously like their father. "You don't think Specter might be a little jittery for her?"

"Lexie's a good rider. Specter will be just perfect." And if he chose the most restive of his own horses, then he'd have enough to think about other than Sexy Lexie. "But are you sure you can trust me? She's a beautiful woman."

Adam laughed. "Neither of us has ever broken the pact. You're hardly about to start now."

Years ago, it had become apparent to the young princes that many of the women they went out with just wanted to date, and possibly marry, a prince. Any prince. If it didn't work out with Adam they made up to Rafe, and vice versa. One wine-sodden evening, the brothers had made a pact to never date a woman the other had dated first. The pact had outlived any and all relationships. So far.

"Besides, she's too serious and too intellectual to interest you." It was as if they were talking about different women. Rafe saw her serious intellectual side, but he also saw the playful, impulsive woman she was, the side she hid from Adam because she didn't think it was regal enough.

"And," Adam announced with the triumph of someone playing a trump card, "she's too young for you."

Rafe just looked at his older brother.

"Spare me the look. I realize that you're closer in age to her. But unlike you, I usually date women younger than me."

"You're right." At least in theory. "But I like her, Adam. And she really wants this to work with you."

"I want it to work, too."

"Then spend some time with her."

"As soon as I can. If Dad hadn't been so hell-bent on getting this under way, it could have been properly scheduled."

Rafe stared at his brother in incomprehension. Properly scheduled? If it was scheduled, you missed the chance of seeing her dancing with her eyes closed, oblivious to the crowd around her, missed seeing her in the moonlight beneath an oak, eyes glittering in the dark, missed the illicit thrill of hearing her laughter as you ran away from a royal dinner with her, missed the surreptitious glances at her as she ran beside you in the gym, ponytail swinging, a droplet of sweat trickling down her chest between her breasts. Instead, his brother wanted to schedule things. Properly.

He studied Adam, could see his mind already weighing solutions to the impending diplomatic problem. "You will do right by her, won't you?"

Adam's eyes widened. "That's a little rich, coming from you, but yes, of course I will. I've planned a dinner for tonight. Something special. Candles, soft music. I'll propose properly, give her the engagement ring I've had made."

Rafe tamped down on a flare of something suspiciously close to jealousy. He'd never felt the emotion before, never thought he'd feel it for Adam, whose life he was only grateful he'd escaped.

"And tonight I'll stay awake for the drive home."

Rafe sat forward. "You'll what? Are you saying you—"

"Fell asleep in the limo on the way back from dinner the other night. Hey," he said with a shrug, as he took in Rafe's stunned expression. "I was tired. It had been a long day."

"You fell asleep?" How did a man fall asleep in Lexie's presence when her proximity had every sense leaping to attention?

"I won't be so tired tonight," Adam said.

Trying to banish thoughts of Adam—not tired—with Lexie, Rafe left.

* * *

Dappled sunlight filtered through the forest canopy. The wooded trail widened, allowing Rafe to urge his mount forward and draw abreast of Lexie. Duke trotted alongside them. Rafe had thought initially that staying behind her, where they wouldn't be able to talk, where he wouldn't see her smile or her green, green eyes, was the better option. But he'd quickly realized that the flare of her hips and the curve of her derriere were a different and possibly worse distraction. He shifted in his saddle.

"This meeting Adam had to go to?" the woman who might one day be his sister-in-law asked. They'd been riding for nearly an hour, and this was the first time she'd brought up Adam's absence, the first time she'd asked anything other than polite questions about the land around them and the flora and fauna of San Philippe.

Her hair was gathered into a lush ponytail that hung down her back. It swept over her shoulder blades when she turned.

"The Global Garden. Someone's bright idea for the anniversary celebrations that has not surprisingly turned into a diplomatic nightmare. Adam has been involved—albeit reluctantly—since its inception. Trust me, he'd much rather be here than there." All three of them would have been happier with that. Particularly Lexie.

"I'd have been happy to ride on my own, or to put it off. Adam has said he'll definitely be free tomorrow." She confirmed his suspicion.

She held the reins lightly in her small, deft hands. Hands a man could imagine touching him. He cleared his throat. "Rain and thunderstorms are predicted for tomorrow."

"Oh."

For a while the only sound was the soft fall of their horses' hooves on the forest floor. She sat so well on Rebecca's gray, moved so in tune with it, that horse and rider looked almost to be one. And he was torturing himself with thoughts of her, thoughts that teetered on the brink of inappropriate or occasionally slipped over that edge. Thoughts that urged him to act. The torture was exquisite and unbearable. Distance. He needed distance.

"I hope it's not too much of an interruption to your day." There was a bite to her tone.

"No," he said evenly. "I ride most days when I'm home."

"So do I," she said with a glimmer of wistfulness and no trace of acerbity.

"You're not sorry you came, are you?" Perhaps she'd go back. He couldn't fathom whether he'd be more relieved or disappointed.

"No, definitely not. I love it here. I just don't want to be in the way." She slid him a look rich with meaning.

"You're not in the way."

"I hear the frustration in your voice."

And if only she knew its real cause. "Don't assume it's because of you."

"You have other sources of frustration?"

"I have sources of frustration you wouldn't believe. Duke," he called back the dog, who had disappeared into the undergrowth.

"What would you have been doing if Adam hadn't asked you to babysit me?" The question was laced with challenge.

"You're far from a baby, Lexie." Far, far from it. "And being with you is not a chore." Except for all the work it entailed in keeping his thoughts in order.

"You're forgetting I heard you use almost exactly those words."

"I was annoyed with Adam at the time. It was nothing to do with you." Which was a lie; it was a lot to do with her, because even back then he'd known that spending time with her was a bad thing for him to do, that there was something different, almost dangerous about her and the way she affected him.

"So, what would you be doing if you weren't filling in for Adam?"

"Nothing," he said casually.

"That's funny, because I saw you in your office earlier."

"When?" He certainly hadn't seen her this morning.

She shrugged. "The middle of the morning. I was on my way back to my room and I passed your office."

"And?"

"And you were inside. At your desk. Talking on the phone and writing something down at the same time. You sounded busy." She shot him a look. "And serious and authoritative even. The glasses were a nice touch, too, very sexy in a scholarly way." She stopped speaking and frowned. "If you like that sort of thing," she added.

Rafe ignored the glasses comment; otherwise he might be tempted to ride back to the palace for a pair. It was true, though, that he'd had dozens of phone calls to make this morning. "Appearances can be deceptive. Maybe I was doodling."

"Doodling?" It was worth it to see her smile like that. "Anyway," she said, "I appreciate you taking time out for me like this."

"You or phone calls and paperwork. It wasn't a difficult choice." It also wasn't a safe choice.

"Was it for the zoo or for the children's ward at the hospital?"

He looked at her.

"I've been trying to find out a little about the work you do. All of you."

"How?"

"I've been talking to Adam's secretary, Martin. He was quite helpful. He told me about the different charities and foundations you all head or are patrons of. The list was massive. He also talked about your personal project to raise money for a hospital gymnasium. And about how you coach and sponsor the polo team you started for the children of palace staff. His son loves it, by the way."

"Martin Junior's one of the best and the keenest players. The kid's always there ahead of time, waiting. No matter how early I get there." Rafe smiled at the thought. "He's all restless energy till you seat him on a horse."

But he didn't want to be talking to this woman about

himself. Didn't want to see or appreciate the warmth of her approval.

He did what he did for his own reasons, lived by his own code as much as that was possible for someone in his position. He'd long since stopped placing importance on anyone else's good opinion. That way he didn't have to worry about disappointing others or being disappointed in return.

"I'd love to come and watch them train." There was a question in her statement.

The fact that he wanted to show her the kids, to show her how good they'd gotten, warned him against that very course of action. "Have Adam bring you along sometime."

She tried to hide her surprise at the rebuff he'd meant to be subtle.

"We each have our charities and other duties." He kept talking to soften the slight. She had to know it was for the best. Unless he was the only one fighting inappropriate thoughts and longings? "I get to choose the fun ones. Adam's duties, as next in line to the throne, tend to be more political than mine."

"He's very diplomatic, isn't he?"

"Yes. And the Global Garden is one he just can't avoid. It's too time sensitive as well as ridiculously politically sensitive. Adam knows all the intricacies and, more important, knows how to calm the waters."

"I understand that. But do you think you could try to explain it to me? In case the workings and considerations involved are the sort of thing I should understand, if, you know…"

If—when—she married Adam and became crown princess. "It's almost incomprehensible to think that it all began two years ago. But that's the way with these things."

She looked at him, her green eyes bright and curious.

"No. I can't explain it." He didn't want her hanging off his words, even if it was for the benefit of his brother. Adam could tell her himself. He could have her looking at him like that. He at least would be able to do something about it. He at least could touch that skin, taste those lips.

"Can't?" Her face clouded over.

"Don't want to." He'd done it again. Proving he wasn't half the diplomat his brother was. He was too blunt, didn't have time for couching messages carefully so that people understood what he meant without upsetting delicate sensibilities. "It's deathly boring." That was as much of a softening as he'd give her. "If you really want to know about it, ask Adam himself. He'll be thrilled that you're interested. Or Martin. I'd only bore us both."

"Maybe I want to be bored."

He hoped Adam appreciated the sacrifices she was making for him. "Maybe I don't want to be the one boring you."

The trail widened further as the forest gave way to a grassy valley. He needed to get some distance and perspective here. If he was going to have to spend time with her, then it would be on his terms.

"Come on." He urged his horse to a canter as

Duke raced ahead. Rafe heard the sound of Lexie's horse behind him, and even more rewarding, a burst of her laughter. She pulled alongside, her expression exhilarated. Surely this was better than boring her. He urged Captain on faster still, up the gentle rise. Lexie stayed by his side. At the top they reined back to a walk. For three hundred and sixty degrees around and below them the palace grounds—forest and farmland—spread out, and beyond that the country of San Philippe itself. On the rise ahead of them stood what remained of an ancient stone church. And now that he had the chance to look behind them, he saw the gathering clouds that the forest canopy had obscured.

Lexie twisted in her saddle to take in the view. "Look. You can see the castle turrets over the treetops. It's all so beautiful. Magical, almost."

So was the glow in her cheeks and eyes. Nothing boring there. "Forecast was out. It's going to rain a whole lot sooner than tomorrow."

She didn't let his pronouncement dampen her enthusiasm. "I love the rain."

She was in some faraway fantasy land. "Even when it's soaking you to your skin?"

She looked at him then. "Not so much then. Unless a warm bath is waiting."

Did she do that deliberately? Conjure up those erotic images? Though in truth, the soaked-to-the-skin one, clothes and hair plastered to her body, blouse all but see-through, was his vision alone. But the bath—the bath image—she was responsible for. He could too easily picture her stepping—bare, slender leg lifted, toes pointed—into a deep, bubble-filled bath, sinking low, letting the heated water rise up her body, over the gentle curve of hips and waist, caressing her breasts.

"Rafe?" she asked, and he got the feeling it might have been the second, if not the third time she'd spoken his name.

He cleared his throat. "Sorry, I was thinking." About you naked. Bad, unbrotherly thoughts about a woman whose only thoughts were about his brother. The twisted mess was surely some kind of divine retribution for earlier misdemeanors.

The first fat drop of rain fell on his hand. It was followed quickly by more. Lexie lifted her face up and closed her eyes, just as she had on the nightclub dance floor, drinking in the pure sensory experience. Would she do that when she made love?

"Come on, we'd better turn back."

"We could shelter in that old church over there."

He followed her gaze to the church. "No. Roof's mostly missing." In truth he didn't think sheltering there alone with Lexie was a good idea. Being alone anywhere with Lexie didn't seem like a good idea. He had to keep his distance and get her back to the palace. No matter what. She was going to dinner with Adam tonight. She wanted to marry Adam. "We're better off heading back. This will blow through quickly enough."

The rain fell more heavily. They were going to get wet. Soaked to the skin, even. It seemed the lesser of two evils.

Rafe urged his horse forward, not looking to see that she followed.

Back at the palace, Rafe led Lexie across the courtyard. Duke's nails clicked quietly on the wet cobbles as he walked beside them. Rafe was almost ready to breathe a sigh of relief. He'd done it. The ordeal was almost over.

Needing to change into dry clothes, they'd left their horses in the care of grooms. The rain had been light and brief. Partially sheltered by the forest canopy, they'd gotten wet, but not soaked. Fortunately.

Or not, depending on your perspective.

Rafe kept his gaze straight ahead as they made their way into the palace, taking a back route to their suites. The fabric of Lexie's blouse wasn't so thin that it was plastered to her body, but it clung in certain places. And it wasn't transparent…precisely. But he knew her bra was pale blue, possibly with white polka dots.

"It must have been fun growing up here," Lexie said as they started up a sweeping staircase. She ran her fingers along the carved, curving balustrade. A caress, almost.

A muted noise that Rafe couldn't quite place sounded somewhere above them. "I guess. Though I didn't always appreciate it." He looked up to the second floor. The art gallery was up there.

"Naturally. You need perspective for that. And you can't get perspective till you've lived somewhere else. Experienced somewhere different."

Like she was changing his perspective on women. Or perhaps the women he'd known before made him appreciate Lexie.

"Did you ever run away?"

"A couple of times. It was pretty difficult. The security staff kept the challenge interesting. You?"

"A few times. I used to hide in the woods. You know, the ones—"

"Yeah. I know." Those same woods he'd found her in. "My specialty was hiding within the palace."

"Really?"

"You don't believe me?"

"You just seem a little...conspicuous."

"Maybe not so conspicuous when I was ten. And parts of this palace are hundreds of years old. There are hiding places galore. Or just places to avoid notice. There's a room at the top of the south turret with views forever, and even to this day it's almost never used." He patted a gleaming suit of armour at the top of the staircase. "The armour was too hard to get into without help. And even if you managed it, you were stuck in it."

"But you tried?"

"Makes an unbelievable racket when you fall over."

Lexie laughed, but Rafe finally placed the other sound he'd been hearing coming from the gallery and growing louder. He muttered a curse.

"What?"

"Schoolchildren. Blasted anniversary. It was in this morning's briefing, but I'd forgotten. Come on." He grabbed her hand, headed along the hallway, past the stern gazes of the portraits hanging on the walls.

Lexie was laughing still. "I didn't know children scared you so much."

"It's not just the children, it's their cameras." His gaze

dipped to her breasts. "I don't think this is the look the royal brand needs right now." And no one else needed to know her bra was pale blue. With white dots.

Her gaze followed his and her eyes widened. "Oh, help. I hadn't realized." Her giggles grew louder.

Duke still at their side, they ran the last few steps to the door he wanted. Rafe reached for the handle just as he heard a high-pitched shout of "Look!" and pulled her into the room, shutting the door behind them. Lexie leaned back against the door, her slender frame shaking with laughter.

Rafe was laughing, too, as his hands slid up, gripping her arms. "Shh." They were making too much noise.

"I'm sorry," she gasped, her mirth brimming over.

His hands reached her shoulders, curved round them. She had no idea what she did to him. How hard he fought her.

"I'm trying." She laughed harder, her eyes dancing. "Really I am."

And Rafe caved in. He stepped closer and covered those laughing lips with his and absorbed her delight as he drank in the taste of her.

Lexie stilled beneath him. A strange, hesitant pause, and then she was kissing him back, swept along with him. Rafe tasted the joy of her. His hands cupped her jaw, fingers sliding into her damp hair, as his tongue learned the sweet, hot ecstasy of her mouth. He felt her growing hunger. A hunger the echo of his own. Felt the heat and fire that was pure Lexie.

It had happened like this at the masquerade ball. The

kiss gathering a life of its own, turning heat to glowing embers to blistering flames in an instant.

He'd known he desired her, but he'd denied it. What he hadn't known enough to even refute was the fathomless depth of that desire. There was no denying it now.

The final shreds of rational thought deserted him as the damp breasts that had tormented him for the last and longest twenty minutes of his life were finally pressed against his chest. The supple length of her molded and moved against him.

He closed his eyes, lost in intoxicating sensation. Hunger and need swamped him as he drowned in the feel of her. Never had anyone's mouth, anyone's body fit so perfectly against his. Never had any woman enflamed his desire as she did. His hunger had him craving. He could kiss her forever and ever and still want to go on tasting and learning her sweet perfection.

His woman. He wanted her. And no one else.

He slid his thigh between hers, felt the exquisite and needy pressure of her as she bore down on him. Rocked, just a little. He slipped his hand beneath her blouse. The cold skin of his palm touched the damp heated curve of her waist. She gasped and froze.

The hands that had been gripping his shoulders suddenly flattened and pushed.

Too late, Rafe remembered with sickening clarity precisely who he was with.

He pulled back, breathing hard. He swallowed, and for once was lost for words. What was he supposed to say? This kiss, unlike their others, had been no accident.

There had been no masks. He'd known precisely who she was as he lowered his mouth to hers.

There had been no thoughts of a peck on the cheek. He'd aimed for her lips.

Officially, only to silence her laughter. But unofficially...that had been an excuse. He'd wanted her kiss. And the instant his lips had touched hers he'd wanted everything from her. All of her.

His brother's woman.

Damn.

Her blouse had slipped from one shoulder, and through his shock he saw that the dots were in fact tiny white daisies. So innocent. A woman who wanted a fairy tale. Which made him the evil villain. He turned away from the distress in her eyes, and away from the reproach in Duke's. And realized he'd led her to a bedroom. That part at least had been unintentional. He strode past the bed to look out the window, giving himself time to gather his thoughts, giving Lexie time to right her blouse and gather her words for the verbal lashing he deserved.

The silence stretched on. Outside, a team of gardeners shoveled mulch around the rose garden. "Lexie, that shouldn't have happened. I shouldn't have done that. I'm sorry."

"So am I." Her quiet voice carried to him. Not angry as she should have been, but distressed. He turned in time to see her striding through the doorway, her blouse hanging loose and untucked at one side.

"Lexie."

She didn't turn, didn't so much as pause or even slow.

<u>Eight</u>

Lexie's hat did little to shade her from the sun beating down on the San Philippe anniversary parade. The cheering, flag-waving crowd, most dressed in the national colors, many in traditional costume, lined both sides of the street.

Feeling like the ultimate fraud, she made her way carefully along the open-topped, double-decker bus that crawled at a snail's pace, bringing up the rear of the parade. The bus carried the royal family and senior dignitaries and a few other guests. But not her mother, who had left early this morning after Lexie's brief conversation with her.

She'd sat beside Adam at the front of the bus for a while, but there was something she had to do, and in public seemed like the safest place.

Her gaze was on the dark head of her quarry as she slid into the empty seat beside Rafe. She hadn't seen or spoken to him since that kiss. He didn't move, though he had to know someone was there. And she figured the very fact that he didn't turn around meant he knew it was her. He just kept waving at an adoring public. Maybe it would be easier to say what she had to if he wasn't looking at her, if she wasn't reading contempt in his eyes. She took a deep breath. "I'm not leaving."

"Seat's free," he said after several seconds. "Doesn't bother me if you sit in it."

Lexie gritted her teeth and then tried again. "I meant I'm not leaving San Philippe."

Rafe glanced over his shoulder at her. "I gathered that much."

"I told Adam about…"

Rafe lifted a hand and waved at the cheering crowds. "I know," he said without looking at her. "So did I."

"He wants me to stay. And I've agreed." She leaned forward to better see his profile. And still knew no more than when she couldn't see his face. He had on his public face, the smiling, pleasant expression he wore in all his publicity shots. The shots that missed the fire and depth of his eyes, and the smile that was a mix of knowledge and temptation.

Maybe his lack of reaction to her news was for the best, because she didn't know whether she wanted him to be pleased or displeased that she wasn't leaving. She didn't, she admitted, know anything at all when it came to Rafe.

His gaze dropped to the unadorned hands in her

lap. She offered no explanation for the lack of a ring. Adam had, in fact, wanted her to have and wear his ring. Lexie hadn't been able to carry the deception that far. But for his sake, though their engagement was off, she'd agreed to stay and be seen with him for one more week. There were joint appearances, like this parade and tomorrow night's Veterans' dinner and dance, that they were committed to, that they would be expected to be seen at.

She'd also agreed to keep their…arrangement a secret. Even from his family. Even from Rafe.

After she left, the news would be released.

A cheer went up somewhere ahead of the bus. The most devoted of the public had waited hours to see this, staking out the positions lining the streets well before the parade began. And prior to the bus's appearance, they'd waited through forty-five minutes' worth of floats and bands and dancers.

Trying to get caught up in the enthusiasm of the waving crowd, and trying to look like she belonged, Lexie waved back. A proper wave, her whole arm moving, none of this sedate hand lifting and twisting of the wrist that most of the royal party thought passed for a wave.

"I fell into your trap. You made your point." She needed Rafe to at least know that she knew what he'd been up to.

"*My* trap?" For the first time he turned and looked at her properly, a frown creasing his brow.

"You said at the outset you'd be watching me, that if you thought I wasn't worthy of Adam you'd do what you could to send me packing. You were trying to prove that

I don't love Adam." In reality he'd only helped speed the decision she would have made anyway.

"We don't need to discuss it," he said sharply.

But she hadn't got to the important bit. She kept her voice low. "I just wanted to say I was sorry."

"*You're* sorry?" He stopped waving and turned to look at her again, those dark brows drawn together.

Fighting the urge to cower beneath the fierceness of his expression, Lexie instead sat straighter. "Yes. I'm apologizing for my part in it."

He shook his head and looked back out at the crowd. "Enough. The fault wasn't yours."

"The weakness was."

"The weakness was mine." He stood, towering over her before he stepped past her. "I've seen someone I need to speak to."

As he walked away, Lexie sagged back into her seat. It was over.

Rafe stood staring absently out one of the ballroom's velvet-curtained, floor-to-ceiling windows. He'd thought his trials were over. He was wrong.

He needed something to take his mind off this test. Because that's clearly what it was. His brother, called into yet another unexpected and unavoidable meeting, had enlisted him to teach Lexie the folk dance, watching him closely for his reaction as he made his request.

Things had, understandably, been strained between Adam and him since he'd kissed Lexie. Though when Rafe had fronted up to Adam about it he'd been surprised at the lack of fire in Adam's annoyance. If their situations had been reversed, he wouldn't have been anywhere near as understanding as his brother.

Of course, Adam, too, thought Rafe had planned and executed the kiss, but in Adam's case he thought it was to teach *him* a lesson. The only consensus they'd reached was in his assurance to Adam that it wouldn't happen again.

But Rafe could do nothing to stop the kiss from replaying itself in his dreams as he slept at night, the touch of her lips to his, the press of her body against his.

It might be easier if either or both Lexie and Adam looked happier. He'd been watching them since Lexie first got here, smiling and doing their best to look like a devoted couple.

Rafe had seen a few devoted couples in his time, and Adam and Lexie didn't even come close. Something wasn't right. Though fortunately the press were buying it. Today's papers had again been filled with photos of Adam and Lexie together. Just one renowned gossip columnist had hinted that she, too, thought their relationship lacked spark.

And now this.

The folk dance might to all appearances be nothing more than a quaint number, but it had its intricacies and its intimacies, and the princes and their partners had to dance it slightly differently from anyone else at the anniversary gala. Or at least that was the story Adam and Rafe had told their respective girlfriends.

And the two of them had, in their day, enjoyed teaching the dance to their dates far too much. They both knew how seductive the held eye contact, the gentle palm-to-palm touches and the story the dance invoked could be.

And now Adam wanted him to teach the dance to Alexia and Rafe had to not seduce or be seduced by her in the process. Wittingly or unwittingly.

Of course it was also possible that Adam was trying to show that he trusted them. Either way, it would still be a trial for Rafe, dancing with the sweet Lexie who was to marry his brother. A man shouldn't have to test his fiancée or his brother, but if Adam needed this, just this, then Rafe would give him that proof. And perhaps he needed it, too.

He turned as Lexie entered the ballroom. Her hair was tied up again—he preferred it that way, it didn't tempt him the way it did when it sat softly over her shoulders, begging to be touched, so that his fingers itched to know the feel of it. She wore a simple silk blouse and a skirt that skimmed the flare of her hips and floated around her calves.

Her hands—her fingers—were still unadorned. Where was Adam's ring? If she were wearing it, that would help; it would be another sign, and he needed all the signs, all the help he could get, to remind him that this woman was not for him.

But for as long as she didn't wear a ring the possible reasons for that lack would taunt and tempt him.

She walked carefully, and Rafe could see in her bearing, her erect posture, her graceful steps, the years of ballet training. He could also see her reluctance to be here with him. "I'm sorry, you have to do this," she said, looking around the cavernous ballroom. "I know you're busy."

"Don't be sorry. I'm not," he lied. No point in her feeling bad, too.

"Yes, you are."

The smile she delivered her accusation with reminded him of the Lexie he'd met that first day in Massachusetts, full of sass. And he realized that his glimpses of that woman were becoming fewer and fewer. Her fault or his?

She was right, of course, about him not wanting to do this, but not for the reasons she suspected. At least he hoped she didn't know the temptation he fought and would go on fighting with every breath he took.

He already had the music for the dance on a loop on the sound system—a flute melody that changed from jaunty to rousing to haunting as it told the story of the two lovers credited with founding the nation of San Philippe and the battles fought between and because of them.

"You know the basic steps?" he asked.

"I learned them as a child, and I found a tutorial on the Internet, but it's not the same as actually dancing it with a partner."

"It's not the same, but it's a simple dance. This won't take long."

She was standing in the center of the ballroom. Sunlight slanted in from the high windows, seeking her out, burnishing her hair. His chosen one.

Rafe banished the thought as he approached her. She stood taller and her hands flexed and clenched at her sides, as though this was some kind of test for her, too.

"And you know the story that the music and the dance tell."

"It used to be my favorite bedtime reading."

He allowed himself a secret sigh of relief. He didn't want to speak to her of the man and woman, at first distrustful of each other, who ended up as lovers meeting clandestinely against their family's wishes, and of how as their families fought, they ran away together, escaping over the Alps and journeying to this land.

"We begin the usual way." Rafe circled her while she stood still, looking straight ahead. The second time he circled her she followed him with her eyes, and the third time, as his shoulder drew level with hers, he held up his palm in a stop gesture and she did the same, touching her palm to his.

That simple touch ricocheted through him. Only, he told himself, because touching her from now on, in any way other than the most formal, was forbidden. *Sister-in-law, sister-in-law,* he repeated the mantra as they moved through the steps, Rafe instructing her, giving her pointers where necessary, keeping his touch as brief as possible.

"You've pretty much got it," he said after ten torturous minutes. "Let's run through it one more time." Just once. He could do that. *Sister-in-law, sister-in-law.* Once and then they'd leave. Then he wouldn't see her or the image of the two of them together reflected in the mirrors on the ballroom walls.

They began again. Holding eye contact they turned

together. Rafe shut down his mind. He just had to get through this. It was a simple dance. Get through it and then get out of here.

Maybe asking him to teach Lexie the dance was neither a test nor a sign of trust, but a punishment. Adam knew Rafe would let nothing happen and he wanted to rub his nose in it.

As the beat of the music changed, they lowered their arms and turned to each other, and he took both of Lexie's hands in his, leaning out, relying on each other for a full rotation. He pulled her closer and then they each stepped back out again. She moved so well, she was so in control of her body. The pale vee of skin at her neckline looked so soft. The curve of her waist, the flare of her hip so tempting. *Sister-in-law, sister-in-law.* He would not be tempted. For a second she closed her eyes, and she could have no idea how that affected him. He'd imagined her, eyes closed, moving with him in a very different way. *Sister-in-law, sister-in-law.* This had to pass. Either that or he'd have to leave the country. Maybe New York? Somewhere he could lose himself. Speculation be dammed.

"Both hands on my shoulders now. And look at me as we step to your left."

He placed his hands at the curve of her waist. Her eyes flew open again and a flush bloomed in her cheeks.

She had eyes of the deepest green. He could lose himself there if he wasn't careful. Two steps to the left. Or Vienna? He could go there. He'd always liked the Austrian capital.

Her foot caught on his as she moved right instead of

left and she stumbled. He tightened his hold reflexively, and for a breath-stealing second the length of her was pressed against him.

They jumped apart and, gazes averted, came warily back together again.

"Sorry," she said, "I wasn't thinking."

"An easy mistake. You've done perfectly otherwise."

"Thank you," she said, her voice as strained and formal as his sounded.

Then silence, except for the delicate teasing music. He could do this—dance with her and not hold her properly, dance with her and not kiss her, dance with her and not want to make love with her.

They were almost finished. Thirty seconds and he'd made it.

He twirled her out and back again so that she finished at his side within the shelter of his arm. As they made the small, courtly bow that signaled the end he sent up a prayer of thanks that this was over.

"We're done?" she asked, her relief palpable.

"Yes. The old soldiers will love you." He stepped away from her, headed for the door.

She passed by him as he held the door for her. This is where he'd say goodbye. And if he could get himself on a plane in a few hours' time, it would be best for all. But if he was leaving, then he only had these few minutes with her.

Being with her was torture, and yet it was better than being without her. And so he walked with her through the palace. Too soon they reached the door to her suite.

All he had to do now was walk away. And he would; he was strong enough for that.

He looked down at her. She was so beautiful it unnerved him. Which was why he was leaving.

A small smile, almost sad, played about her lips, but her eyes drank him in. He recognized that hunger—it was the echo of his own. "Don't look at me like that. I'm only human, Lexie."

She backed away, crossed her arms as she shook her head. "I wasn't looking at you…like that."

"Yes, you were. You want me."

Her jaw dropped open.

"It's nothing more than the truth. And if you're looking at me like that, why are you marrying my brother?" The brother who liked and respected her, but who didn't love her, not with the kind of love she deserved, the love she'd dreamed of for so many years.

She paused, didn't quite meet his gaze. "Adam is a good, kind, honorable man," she said, not quite answering his question.

"You forgot noble and sweet."

"You're right. Noble and sweet."

"And nice."

"Yes. Nice."

"So, why do you think about me?"

"I don't."

"Yes, you do. You watch me and you think about me. You think about me touching you." He lifted his hand, touched fingertips to her jaw. A tremor shivered over his skin and her eyelids fluttered closed. With a gasp, she turned her head and stepped away from his touch.

"You're the last man on earth I'd think about."

Who did she think she was fooling? Rafe took a step closer. She took another away from him, stopping as her back pressed against her door.

A sliver of air separated them, and it hummed with his need for her. "First and last, and all the ones in between."

"No." She whispered her denial through softly parted lips.

"Marrying Adam is a mistake. For you. For him." He could see the rise and fall of her breasts as she drew in shallow, ragged breaths. "Don't do it."

"No. I'm not," she whispered.

Her response didn't quite make sense, but the pull of her overwhelmed him. He was leaving. For forever if he had to. But heaven help him he was going to kiss her.

Just once more.

One kiss to prove she shouldn't marry his brother, one kiss to prove he was as depraved as the tabloids painted him.

He lowered his head, his face so close to hers that her breath caressed his lips. Whatever happened, whether he kissed her or not, he couldn't win; he would regret the decision for the rest of his life.

Lexie closed her eyes. So young. So innocent.

Calling on reserves of strength he didn't know he had, Rafe pulled away.

Her eyes flew open, locked on his for a timeless second. He tried and failed to back away. "I'm not marrying Adam." Her words rushed out. And suddenly it was her hands in his hair, pulling him down, and Lexie rising up to him, pressing her lips to his.

Her mouth fitted perfectly against his. She tasted of sweetness and sunshine. For long, exquisite moments there was just that simple joining, lips to lips and somehow soul to soul.

He broke the kiss. "Say that again." He needed the words that made sense of everything.

"I'm not marrying Adam. We broke it off." She reached for him again and her kiss was everything he needed and wanted in the world. She was his perfection.

Still kissing her, he moved with her into her room, shut the door behind them. Lexie sighed against him as she melted into him, an echo of his own surrender.

And he lost himself in her kiss.

Thought deserted him, overwhelmed by sensation.

"When?" he finally asked, minutes later.

"After I kissed you the last time. I knew then that—"

He pulled her against him, hip-to-hip, her yielding softness against his hardness. His hands desperately learning her shape, sliding beneath the silk of her blouse, touching heated skin smoother than the silk, tracing her contours, the flare of her hips, the curve of her waist, filling himself with the feel of her, her taste, her scent. Imprinting her against him, within him.

Her tongue danced with his, an erotic twining as they each teased and explored. Nothing sweet, all heated desire. He cupped the soft weight of her breast, his thumb caressing the lace-covered nipple.

"Why?" He heard his own doubt. Felt his desperation.

She hesitated. "Because I don't love him. I can't love him. Not the way I want to."

Could it be the insanity telling him he heard the words he needed to hear? The relentless grip of his ungovernable need for her? He undid the top button of her blouse.

"He was very gracious about it."

Showed what a fool his brother could be.

"I think he was secretly relieved."

Not half as relieved as Rafe was. He undid the second delicate button. "Why are you still here?"

"For Adam."

He frowned, his fingers stilling on the third button. "You do still have feelings for him?"

"No. I told him I'd stay and attend any engagements I'm expected at. If I left so soon it wouldn't look good. There would be all sorts of speculation. I leave after the christening."

Rafe's hands resumed their exploring.

"It turns out he was mainly going through with this to please your father and the country. Apparently, a wedding, any royal wedding, will be good for the country's morale. Funny how no one thought to mention that to me."

"You're not angry with him?"

She shrugged and he felt the movement beneath his fingertips. "I was hardly in a position to take the moral high ground."

He undid the fourth and final button and, with a

profound sense of achievement and victory, pushed apart the sides of her blouse, revealing a strip of creamy skin and partially uncovering the swell of lace-covered breasts.

His breath caught in his throat.

He arranged the blouse to his liking and traced a finger along the edge of the lace. "Why didn't you tell me sooner?"

"Because I didn't want this to happen."

He paused. "Why are you telling me now?"

"Because now...now I want this to happen. I can't bear it any longer. The wanting you. I didn't break up with him because of you. We're supposed to be keeping it a secret, but..."

He didn't need buts. She wasn't engaged to his brother, and the realization filled him with euphoria, swamped any other thought.

He cupped her sweet face in his hands and kissed her again. He could no more have stopped himself than he could from taking his next breath. He wanted to know her, every inch of her.

She wasn't marrying Adam. She didn't love his brother. His brother didn't love her. That was all he needed to know.

Wrapping his arms around her, he held her to him, drowning in the sensation of her, in the shape of her and how she fit against him, body and mouth and soul.

Her hands slid from his shoulders to his head, her fingers threading through his hair, her touch becoming fevered.

He kissed her lips, her eyes, her jaw, her throat. His

hands learned the exquisite shape of her body as he led her to the broad bed in the center of the room. He eased the sides of her blouse farther open, kissed her breast above the lace of her bra, moved lower till his lips covered the nipple beneath the lace.

Sweet Lexie arched into him.

He pushed her blouse from her shoulders. Her skin was so pale, so beautiful. He found the single button at the back of her skirt, a short zip, and the fabric slithered to the floor. She stood before him in delicate scraps of lace and her shoes.

Almost perfect.

He unpinned her hair, let it cascade over his hands as it came loose. He undid the clasp of her bra and her breasts spilled free. He tossed the lace aside and then drew her panties down her legs. Breathless, he looked at her, his fantasy complete.

Now she was perfect.

And Rafe was both honored and humbled.

Her lips curved into a slow, sensuous smile. With just a touch of hesitancy she reached for his belt. Urgency replaced the hesitancy as she worked the buckle and then the button and zipper behind it.

He pulled his top off, stepped out of his shoes and the pants she'd pushed down his legs. He held himself still while those pale, delicate hands of hers explored his torso, lighting sparks with her curious, reverent touch.

Demure Lexie was his siren. Bold, beautiful. Smiling. Her hair whispering over her shoulders.

He could bear it no longer. He scooped her up and lowered her down onto the bed. Where he'd wanted this woman from the moment he saw her dancing in the nightclub. He raised her arms above her head, captured her wrists in one hand so that his other was free to caress and slide and cover and tease. And to claim. Every inch. Sliding his hand up one pale thigh to her apex, he covered her and she arched into his hand. She closed her eyes, as he'd imagined, as he'd dreamed.

He found her center and took delight in her pleasure and her growing need till her head swung from side to side, her breathing ragged.

The only thing he wanted was to give her pleasure.

He covered her lips again with his and moved his body over hers. She parted beneath him, welcomed him as he slid slowly into the depth of her, sheathing himself in her heat. She opened her eyes then, and her gaze locked on his as he began to move within her.

Slowly. He should take it slowly, but she moved beneath him, urging him faster, her hips rising to meet his thrusts, the hands he'd freed now clasping his hips, pulling him in deeper.

Little moans and mewls of pleasure escaped her, driving him out of his mind with need for her. Along with the spiraling need, a rhythm that was theirs alone grew and hastened. All the world narrowed down to this one joining. Her with him.

As she cried out his name, he lost himself in her.

Afterward, she lay within the circle of his arms, her hair auburn and beautiful spilling over the pillow, across his shoulder, its faint floral scent teasing his senses. As Rafe watched her, a strange sense of bliss settled over him.

Nine

Lexie stood between Adam and Rebecca in the royal enclosure, trying to enjoy the anniversary fireworks display. As per their arrangement, she'd stayed at Adam's side through yet another formal dinner and for the last half hour out here. And still she'd been constantly aware of Rafe.

Rafe, whom she'd slept with.

She watched a series of starbursts of color and noise. As dandelions blossomed in the night sky, she heard the oohs and ahhs of the gathered crowd. But from the corner of her eye she watched Rafe. More riveting than the fireworks.

Among the royal guests were the young teens from Rafe's polo team, whom he'd promised this treat to if they won their last match. They had. Convincingly.

He was great with the kids and they clearly idolized him, the boys and girls alike. They listened avidly to what he said and tried hard to impress him. And he seemed to give them just the right amount of attention and encouragement back. Not too much, not too little. For someone who didn't want a relationship, he'd make a great dad. And that was not a thought she should be having.

As he crouched to speak with an older man in a wheelchair, her thoughts began to wander.

She hadn't seen him since she'd left her bed yesterday afternoon to shower.

Sanity had returned after the desperation of their lovemaking. They'd agreed, as they'd lain together, legs entwined, Rafe stroking her hair, touching her face, that it couldn't be allowed to happen again. That, in fact, they'd pretend that it had never happened in the first place.

It was the only sensible course of action. No matter how hollow the decision had made her feel.

A failed engagement with Adam was bad enough. A relationship with Rafe, the Playboy Prince, even if it never became public, could only be catastrophic, on so many levels.

He'd been gone by the time she came back out from her shower. Today she'd had back-to-back engagements. Mostly with Adam. During all of which she had thought about Rafe.

And missed him.

Rafe, who'd made no attempt to contact her. She knew he wouldn't, because they'd agreed that was best.

And the fact that she'd wanted him to only made her a fool.

She'd half hoped, as she gave herself to him, that he would be a disappointment. Because there was no future in a relationship with Rafe. They wanted different things.

But he hadn't been a disappointment. He'd been a revelation. An insanity. Ecstasy and bliss. He'd been overwhelming passion. Infinitely more than her meager imagination had conjured.

"How are things going with Adam?" Rebecca asked.

"Fine," she said hesitantly. Not wanting to discuss Adam with Rebecca. Not wanting to carry the deception any further than she had to. "Who's Rafe talking to?"

Rebecca followed her gaze and smiled. "Malcolm. He was our head groundsman for decades. Such a lovely man. It's so hard to see him like this. He and Rafe had a really special bond. Rafe was so active, always needing to be doing something, and Malcolm had the patience to teach him practical skills as well as a love of the outdoors to share. It all started with the tadpoles and frogs he used to find for Rafe in the lily pond."

Lexie smiled at the thought. "I used to call Rafe the Frog Prince. Ever since that time I was eight and he threw a frog at me."

Rebecca laughed. "Rafe went through such a phase with them. And turtles. That particular frog was one of the last generation in a long line of frogs he'd had since he was a little kid. He even had a name for it. Arnold or something."

"Arthur."

"That's it. Dad had told us to think of something nice for you on that visit. That frog was the best Rafe could think of. He wanted to show it to you. Thought that an eight-year-old girl would have been as interested as he'd been when he was eight. Adam and I tried to tell him it wasn't the thing, but he wasn't having it. Then Adam knocked him and it fell into your lap."

"Adam knocked him? I thought Rafe threw it."

Rebecca was still smiling. "I remember the pandemonium. Us all on our hands and knees searching for it. Dad had a fit. Rafe had to put it out in the pond after that. In fact, he was banned from frogs thereafter."

Lexie had to rewrite the entire incident in her head. Her Frog Prince. It had been a small thing, but pivotal in her admiration of Adam and her dislike of Rafe. For an eight-year-old, she'd been able to hold a powerful grudge.

And she'd had it all wrong.

He hadn't been trying to torment her. He should have been the one with the grudge. Because of her, he'd lost his pet. Though she couldn't help thinking Duke was a vast improvement.

Rebecca looked back in Rafe's direction. "It's so nice that Adelaide, Malcolm's granddaughter, is home for the summer now, to help look after him. She got back just a couple of days ago."

Lexie looked at the woman behind Malcolm. She was the same woman she'd seen Rafe talking to in a doorway just a few nights ago. Her heart sank. This was the woman she'd more or less implied he was having an illicit relationship with. Adelaide lifted her sunglasses from her eyes and Lexie realized just how young she was, still a teenager. A handsome youth approached and slung his arm around Adelaide's shoulders and the girl blushed. And Lexie was racked with yet more guilt. She'd all but accused Rafe of having an affair with the young woman, thinking herself worldly as she did so. She was as bad as the tabloids. And Rafe had done almost nothing to defend himself or correct her assumption. He'd said there was nothing going on and she hadn't believed him.

She'd done him such a disservice, thinking the worst of him, believing his tabloid reputation when she should have known better. There was so much more to him than the picture the press liked to paint of him. He let people believe the worst of him, when clearly he was so much better than that.

And here in public, with camera lenses trained on the whole royal party, she couldn't go to him and apologize. Nor could she go to him in private. The risk there was entirely different and far graver.

She couldn't go to him at all. It was her only option.

Lexie looked in horror from the newspapers spread out on her bed, to the card in her hand, to the phone beside her and then back to the papers.

Staying away from Rafe was not an option now. She had to do this. Taking a deep breath, she reached for the phone and slowly dialed the number.

Three rings. It was too early to be calling. But she

couldn't leave it and risk missing him. Four rings. One more and she'd hang up.

"Rafe." A single rough syllable.

Her throat dried up.

"Who's there?" he asked, a little more gently, but still with a husky, sleep-filled inflection. "Lex?"

"I'm sorry. I didn't mean to wake you. I can call again later." She tried not to recall the image of him sprawled and slumberous in this very bed.

"I'm awake now. What's wrong?"

"Aside from the fact that we slept together?" She looked again at the pictures in the papers.

Silence.

"Can I see you? It's the papers."

"To which you should pay no attention."

"Please? You should see this. I don't know what to do about it. I mean, I know I have to tell Adam, but I thought you should see it first. That was all."

A ray of sunlight slanted through her window, highlighting the very picture she needed to show him. Outside, she heard the notes of the mockingbird whose bachelor's song had disrupted her sleep throughout the night.

"You know where my office is?"

"Yes." His office was relatively neutral territory, nice and official, not tempting.

"Can you be there in twenty minutes?"

"Yes. Thank you."

When she got there, she waited outside the door to Rafe's office and forced herself to stand still. She'd pulled on the first clothes to hand, jeans and a white blouse, and come straight here. She was at least five minutes early, undoubtedly a mistake because now she was loitering in the corridor where any of the staff or family, if they were up, could see her and wonder what she was doing, why she was waiting for Rafe. Had gossip already spread through the castle? As far as she knew no one had seen them, but…

She clutched this morning's San Philippe paper and yesterday's American paper in her hands. Both had been delivered early to her room, as they had been every day she'd been here. The first had caused her to spill her coffee, the second to forget her coffee altogether. She'd only looked at each once before quickly closing them. And she hadn't yet dared check the Internet.

Her first panicked impulse had been to call Rafe. Not only because her predicament involved him, but because he'd know what to do. He'd dealt with scandals before, and for the first time she could see some benefit in that.

And like her, he didn't want his brother to be hurt.

She was on the verge of walking away, planning to come back shortly, when Rafe strode down the corridor. His hair was damp, and his white linen shirt revealed a vee of tanned skin. He wore black jeans and he looked masculine and earthy. The sort of man her mother had warned her about. She should have listened. But more important, she told herself, he looked calm and capable. Some of her anxiety eased. She'd made the right decision. He'd know what to do, how she should handle this.

"Lex," he said by way of a greeting. She wasn't sure

whether she imagined the same longing in his voice that she was unable to quell. For all the lectures she'd given herself, she still thought about him, dreamed about him.

His gaze traveled leisurely over her, and she had to hide the physical reaction, the leap of her pulse, that his presence inevitably caused. His eyes seemed to linger on her hair, which because of her distraction still lay loose around her shoulders. A frown creased Rafe's brow and he swallowed. Clearly she should have taken the time to put it up. She remembered too well how much he loved her hair, how he had run his fingers through it, arranged it over her shoulders, her chest.

"I'm sorry about this," she said, clutching the papers tighter. "I didn't want to bother you. I just didn't know who else to ask for advice. And you did give me your phone number and say to call. This isn't about a fork or anything, but it concerns you, too."

He turned from her and tapped a code into the keypad by the door. After pushing it open he stood aside for her to enter. "You can call me anytime, Lex. You don't need to apologize."

She stepped past him. She'd seen his office once before, a glance as she'd passed by, but she hadn't had a good look at it, partly because her attention had been caught by the man who'd occupied it.

She looked now. It was a beautiful room, dominated by a massive, intricately carved desk, its surface clear of anything. The paperwork that had covered it the time she'd seen him in here working was nowhere in sight.

The walls were lined with floor-to-ceiling book-filled shelves. Plush carpet cushioned her footsteps as she crossed to the window she knew to be bulletproof. A view over the palace grounds and beyond to the rolling farmland and forest greeted her. And in the distance, golden sunlight bathed mountaintops still capped with snow.

"How bad is this situation?" he asked. "Do I need to close the door?"

Lexie turned at the reluctance in his voice. He still stood by the door, watching her. She hesitated. "No. I don't think so." A closed door would be bad. That would suggest she—they—had something to hide. And it could also too easily lead to temptation.

"Sit down—" he gestured to one of the leather chairs in front of his desk "—and tell me what's wrong."

As he spoke he crossed to his desk and sat behind it. He looked remote and strained, not the friend she'd thought she had in him. But remote was good. Remote worked for her. She could have friendship with Adam and Rebecca. For now all she needed was to let Rafe know what had happened and get his opinion and his advice.

She'd be gone from here soon. He, on the other hand, would have to stay and deal with the fallout. Lexie put the newspapers on the desk. He smoothed out the creases her clutching had caused. And she remembered those hands on her body. To distract herself, she turned over the first page of the San Philippe Times. Rafe raised his eyes to hers briefly before scanning the page before him.

It was covered almost entirely in the story of her

supposed engagement to Adam. There was one picture of her unadorned left hand and some speculation as to the possible reason for the delay in the appearance of a ring.

"This was expected," he said. "There'll be more when the news that you're going home—permanently—breaks, but then that, too, will pass. Something bigger always eventually comes along."

As bothered as she was by all the talk of an engagement that no longer existed, that wasn't why she was here. "Bottom right photo. The one of you."

His gaze tracked to the photo in question.

"And...me. Together." It had been taken in the nightclub in Boston. And it looked like he was holding her to him. His lips were close to her ear. It looked intimate. Nothing like what had really been happening. Although Lexie clearly recalled how it had felt, how even then her brain had fired off frantic warning signals that she hadn't fully understood about the unfortunate chemistry Rafe caused to spark into life.

"And could an engagement be in the offing for our other prince?" he read the caption aloud. The small piece went on to answer its own question, speculating that this was just the latest dalliance for a man with more than his share of oats to sow. It asked when the second prince was going to grow up and settle down. It listed Rafe's previous girlfriends and then went on to wonder at the identity of the mystery woman.

A tap sounded at the door and it opened slightly. Rafe nodded for a woman in the palace staff uniform, carrying a silver tray with two coffees, to come in.

He waited till she'd left again. "I didn't know whether you'd had time for your coffee."

"I started one, but I spilt it." She pointed out the stain on the second paper.

Rafe passed her the coffee, made just how she liked it.

"Thank you."

He sat and leaned back in his chair, swiveling to look out the window as he sipped his own coffee.

"What should we do?"

He took his time answering. "I know I said I didn't think that picture would make it to the papers, and clearly I was wrong. But I really don't think anyone's going to recognize you. Your face is largely obscured, and you really didn't look like you. I only recognized you that night because I was there. Looking at this—" he tapped the paper "—if I didn't know it was you, I wouldn't guess it. You're safe."

"But you?"

His frown deepened.

"They've got it all wrong, suggesting it was something it's not. They're tarnishing your reputation, and bringing up all your earlier girlfriends."

"Tarnishing my reputation?" He sat back in his chair and laughed. "My reputation is so blackened a little tarnish isn't going to show. And as for *all* my other girlfriends—" he glanced back at the list "—I'd scarcely have had time for even half of the women mentioned."

"It doesn't make you angry?"

"Why waste the emotion on something I can't change?

Like I said, some other news will come along and this will be forgotten."

"What about Adam and your father?"

"What about them?"

"I thought maybe if I explained it to them?"

Rafe smiled. "To save my reputation?"

"Well, yes." It sounded silly.

The smile softened, and a curious expression lit his eyes. "No," he said slowly. "All you'd do is damage your own. And for no good reason. We both know what that was and wasn't."

She couldn't figure him out. "Why do you let people think the worst of you? You did it with Adelaide and the frog and you're doing it now."

"The frog?"

"Arthur. Back when I was eight. I thought you threw him at me. That Adam had rescued me. I was so upset with you about it, and I'm sorry."

"Lex, it was fourteen years ago. It doesn't matter."

"It must have mattered then."

"Even if it did, it certainly doesn't now."

"I used to call you the Frog Prince."

He laughed, that rumble that started in his chest. "So that's why you kissed me. To see if I'd turn into a prince."

She laughed, too. "Like you weren't already one to start with." Though it really had taken her a while to see that. "I'm sorry, anyway."

"For what?"

"For believing the worst of you."

His smile was gentle. "You're too sweet for this life,

Lex. If you let what other people think get to you they'll hurt you even if they don't mean to."

Just like she cared what he thought about her, and was doubtless going to be hurt by him even though he wouldn't mean to?

Holding her gaze, he folded the paper and pushed it across the desk toward her.

Uncomfortable under his scrutiny, she felt sillier than ever. "So I should just say nothing?"

"'No comment,' particularly when you haven't even been asked for one, is your greatest friend. But the pictures aren't the real question."

She wasn't going to ask.

"Us," he said.

Lexie couldn't hold his gaze for fear of what she might reveal, so she looked out the window at the bright morning. For a moment she let herself entertain thoughts of the possible answers, possible outcomes. But in the end she gave the only answer she could. "Same strategy as for the pictures," she said, pretending nonchalance. That's what he'd want from her. No drama. "Ignore it. I'll be gone soon and we won't even have to see each other. There is no us. That's what we agreed."

"And that's still how you want to play it?"

He gave no hint of the sentiment behind the neutral question, but she was guessing relief. "Unless you can think of a better way that doesn't involve hurting anyone."

"You mean Adam?"

And her. But she didn't say that. "It's going to be bad enough when news of the broken engagement gets out. Can you imagine if anyone gets wind that you and I…"

"That we what?"

He was going to make her say it. "That we slept together."

"Is that all it was?"

What was he playing at? "Of course that's all it was. Just something we apparently needed to get out of our systems."

"And did you? Get me out of your system?"

"Yes." She might be a liar, but she wasn't a fool. And if she admitted that sleeping with Rafe had done nothing to get him out of her system, rather had only shown her a deep pleasure and ecstasy she hadn't known existed, that even now the needy physical part of her wanted him, wanted him just to hold her even, then he'd feel obliged to gently point out that they could never have a future.

She'd save them both that excruciating exchange.

This was the only way to play it. The only way to emerge unscathed.

As dawn began to win out over darkness, Lexie got up. It was no hardship when, after the nightmare yesterday had turned into, she hadn't been sleeping anyway. She made her way through the maze of palace corridors, passing only a handful of quietly observant staff members whose expressions revealed nothing of what they thought, what they knew.

Outside, she took the path through the dew-covered rose gardens, too preoccupied to stop and smell them. The path led her, eventually, to the labyrinth.

A place of meditation and thought. A place to seek answers. She'd walked it once already a few days earlier. That time had been out of curiosity. This time she felt the need for its reputed calming and problem-solving benefits—the labyrinth's famed metaphorical journey within.

She watched the path as she entered the circling waist-high hedges of the labyrinth and listened to the quiet crunch of her own footsteps on the gravel. After the first quarter circle the path turned back on itself and then took her deceptively toward the center. It was only then that she looked up at the spreading oak tree there.

Still and watching her from the bench that encircled the tree sat Rafe. Lexie didn't so much as break her stride and she certainly didn't turn and leave, much as she suddenly wanted to. Instead, she kept putting one foot in front of the other, following the path. She had to keep passing and re-passing in front of his line of sight, near to him and then far. She didn't look to see whether he was watching her, but he was. She didn't need to look to know it. She could feel it.

With all the turning back and circling, it took her a strangely long time to reach him, and then there was nothing else to do but sit beside him. Duke lay at his feet and lifted his head as she sat. "I didn't realize you were here when I started."

"That much was obvious from the doe-in-the-headlights look in your eyes when you first saw me." She heard the smile in his voice.

"I don't want to interrupt this time for you."

"You're no interruption, Lex." Did he know he was the only one who called her that? He reached for one of the hands curled into fists on her lap, straightened her fingers and then enfolded her hand in his.

The sight and sensation of their joined hands pierced something within her. As she made to extricate her hand, his grip tightened. "I thought we weren't going to…"

"What? Hold hands? I thought we weren't going to sleep together again."

"We're not sleeping together again."

"Then I'm holding your hand. There's no one here to see us. And it would be pleasanter if you didn't make a big deal about it. It fits so well in mine."

Lexie didn't answer, didn't argue. It did fit well, like the most natural thing in the world.

She closed her eyes and leaned back and thought of everything that had happened since this man first took her hand on the croquet lawn back home and kissed it. So much, too much, and yet not enough.

She'd thought yesterday's papers were something to worry about. Today's were far worse.

"How did the meeting with your father go?" Yesterday Prince Henri had seen advance copies of today's papers. News of the end of her engagement to Adam had broken like a dam bursting. No one knew where the leak had come from. It didn't really matter now. Speculation was beginning on the Internet that somehow Rafe was involved. He'd told her of his summons to see his father and let her know that he'd be telling his father as much of the truth as he thought he needed to know. She hadn't asked precisely how much that involved.

"He demanded that I marry you. He always does whenever I'm involved in a scandal. He thinks a big royal wedding will go a long way to fixing things."

"Oh." It hurt that he could be so blasé. That suddenly she was just one of his many scandals. "What did you say to him?"

"That I'd live my life according to my own dictates, not his."

"Oh." It was exactly what she'd known he would say. She'd never have married him just to please his father anyway, so there was no reason for the feeling of loss.

"Adam joined in the lecture, too. He's very protective of you."

"I'm sorry."

"Don't be. You were worth it."

Were? Past tense.

His thumb rubbed gently over the back of her hand.

"Did you hear from your mother?" he asked a short while later.

"Yes. I let her know that the rumors were starting and that they weren't totally unfounded." Suddenly pictures were appearing of every public exchange she'd had with Rafe, and somehow they all managed to look charged and intense. Probably because they had been.

"How did she take it?"

"Let's just say that, whatever happens, one of our parents is going to be bitterly disappointed."

"Let me guess. She demanded that you never see me again."

"That's pretty much it."

"And what did you tell her?"

"I thought of you, and of how you'd react if someone told you what to do, and I told her that I was old enough to decide for myself who I saw and who I didn't."

"Good for you."

"And then I kind of spoiled it by telling her that I'm coming home the day after the christening, anyway. I could go sooner, but it would feel like running away. And Adam and your father have both asked me to stay. I'm not sure why. Something to do with Marconis and Wyndhams never backing down from a challenge, and a strong offence being the best form of defense. And they mentioned dignity, too. They kind of lost me, but I said I would stay." Rafe was the only one who hadn't asked her to stay.

Even now he said nothing. Not that she expected a pleading, heartfelt *don't go, stay with me forever* from this man, but a girl was allowed her daydreams. Lexie shook her head. She of all people should have learned her lesson about daydreams and fantasies and fairy tales.

"You've had a miserable time here, haven't you?"

"No, it's—"

"Have you done anything just for you, just for the sheer enjoyment of it?"

"That wasn't the purpose of the trip."

Shaking his head he stood and pulled her up with him. "Come on." He started walking.

"What? Where?"

"If we can't please both of our families then let's

annoy them both. And really give the press something to talk about."

"What do you mean?" He was leading so fast through the labyrinth she was getting dizzy.

"Do you trust me, Lexie?"

"No." She had no idea what he was planning, but was almost certain she wasn't going to like it. And yet she hurried along beside him, her heart beating faster in exhilaration and anticipation.

He laughed, turned back and planted a quick hard kiss on her lips. "Wise woman."

Forty minutes later, Lexie strapped herself into the seat next to Rafe, their shoulders touching.

"Ready?" he asked.

"No." She gripped his hand.

"Too bad." Photographers ran toward them, snapping pictures as the roller coaster of San Philippe's only theme park began to gather speed and then shot them forward. Lexie managed not to scream until they were out of sight.

The photographers were still there, a hungry pack of them, snapping away as the roller coaster eased to a stop. Lexie's hair had come free from her hair tie, helped, she suspected, by Rafe, and must surely look a fright.

Her mother would be appalled.

Lexie laughed at the prospect, suddenly not caring what people thought. Suddenly appreciating Rafe's philosophy.

The photographers followed them, at a distance, almost all day long. Taking pictures of the most mundane of things. Walking, talking, laughing, Rafe winning her a teddy bear in a shooting booth. It was all so clichéd. And all so much fun.

The only privacy they got was when Rafe managed to get a quiet booth in the riverside café where they stopped for dinner, the proprietor fiercely denying entry to anyone with a camera.

At the nightclub he took her to they danced till the small hours of the morning.

By the time Lexie fell into bed—alone—she was exhausted but happy. It was the best day she could remember, well, ever. Even with the repressed pall of sorrow that everything was ending. They'd talked of the present, never the future. Because, she knew, Rafe didn't do futures.

Ten

Amongst a sea of talking and laughing christening guests, Rafe reluctantly took hold of the baby. He was happy to be godfather—Mark and Karen were good friends—but why did people always expect that he'd want to hold their children? Although maybe godfathers ought to want to. Lex would doubtless have an opinion on the subject. Lex, whom he did want to hold, but couldn't and wouldn't because she was leaving tomorrow, going back to her old life. It was for the best.

They'd had yesterday, undoubtedly a mistake given the outcry in the media. But a mistake he couldn't regret. He'd wanted it to last forever, wanted her smiles and her laughter.

He looked into the clear blue and strangely alert eyes of the child in his arms, who appeared, much like Rafe, to be wondering why this strange man was holding her. Karen called to someone across the room and walked away, and Rafe had to stop himself from calling her back.

"If you cry now," he quietly encouraged the child whose name he'd already managed to forget, "your mother will come back for you." In Rafe's experience, that was how this scenario usually played out. Unfortunately, this child didn't know the drill and merely blinked. He was fairly sure she was a girl, though that long gown she, or he, had worn for the cathedral ceremony wasn't necessarily a guarantee of femininity.

Conversation flowed around him, and the baby continued to study him. "I hold you responsible," he said, and the baby smiled. "If it hadn't been for this christening, I could have been in Vienna by now. Or maybe even Argentina." And he wouldn't have entangled his life and emotions with Lexie. Although he couldn't bring himself to regret what they'd shared.

The baby's stare turned accusing.

"Okay," he admitted. "I stayed for her, too. But don't you dare tell anyone."

He heard a bubbling, sexy laugh and followed the sound to Lexie, where she stood talking with Adam and Karen. She wore a silky red wrap dress. He'd been pleased to see her in it. Pleased and turned on, but he ignored the second reaction. She'd at least stopped trying to hide her vibrancy behind fiercely elegant clothes. No point now, he guessed, given that she wasn't marrying his brother. She was leaving. Her hair was pulled into a twist at the back of her head, its lushness contained.

That fact pleased him, too. He admitted to a proprietary attitude to her hair—it featured in so many of his fantasies.

She caught him watching her. Her gaze dipped to the baby in his arms and her eyes widened in surprise. *Yes, Lexie,* he thought, *I do know how to hold a child, it's just not something I do voluntarily.* And Lexie was exactly the sort of woman who'd want children, who'd be a natural, loving mother. Which was why he had to let her go.

He looked around for Karen. Surely he'd done his godfatherly duty and could hand the baby back. And leave. "Okay, kid, where's your mother?" Only now the child had closed its eyes and—he couldn't believe it— gone to sleep in his arms. It was the strangest feeling. He held the warm bundle a little closer.

"You're in trouble now." He heard a soft, smiling voice at his side.

"Meaning?" he asked Lexie, wanting only to hand the baby away so he could fill his arms with this woman instead. Yes, he was in trouble all right.

"I understood you have a policy of never falling asleep with a woman, and I'm figuring that extends to letting them fall asleep in your arms." She spoke quietly, her words winding sensuously around him.

"First time for everything."

She touched her fingertip gently to the sleeping child's cheek.

"You want children?" he asked, even though the answer was obvious in the softness of her smile, in the tenderness and longing that lit her face.

"Someday. Doesn't everyone?" The smile widened with secret thoughts and plans.

"No. Not everyone."

"Like Everest?"

"Exactly." He smiled back, enthralled, held captive by what felt like an almost physical connection to her. The entire roomful of people could fade away and he wouldn't notice. She felt it, too. This wasn't one-sided. Which only made the situation worse.

"But don't you? Want children." She searched his face.

"It's not something I've thought about." And he was terrified that looking at her, children were something he could want. "Here, do you want to hold her?" He nodded at the soundly sleeping little girl. If Lexie was holding the baby, she'd stop looking at him. And the sight of her holding a baby would stop him thinking thoughts he shouldn't. He couldn't possibly lust after a woman holding an infant. It would just be wrong.

"Emma?"

That was her name, of course.

"Yes, please."

He passed the sleeping child to Lexie. They had to stand close, almost chest to chest, only Emma between them, hands bumping and sliding.

"Babies aren't your thing?" Lexie asked, not looking at him, as she took Emma's weight, held her to her chest.

"Not at all." His standard answer came to him. And yet he'd felt the strangest reluctance to let go of the small bundle. The child who had fallen asleep in his arms.

"You'll be a great father. Once you give yourself permission to love," she said. "It doesn't have to be scary."

Oh, but it was.

She couldn't leave soon enough. It was torture seeing her. Seeing her hope, her optimism.

As Karen approached, Rafe took a flute of champagne from a passing waiter. He saw one of his few remaining bachelor friends and headed to talk to him. Preferably about polo or something equally safe, equally shallow.

Lexie rested her hands on the rough stone of the windowsill and looked out through the tall, narrow window. The day room was at the top of the castle's southernmost turret. Rafe had mentioned it once, mentioned its forever views and its isolation. After navigating corridors and climbing endless winding stone stairs, Lexie could see why it was so was so seldom used. But the views over the manicured palace grounds and the rolling countryside beyond were worth the effort. The sky was a clear, bright blue, taunting her. It should be dreary and miserable to match her mood.

The room was just as she'd imagined. A contrast of textures and centuries. Leather couches, shaped to fit the circular space, lined the small room. A plush rug lay in the center of the floor.

She'd escaped the christening, escaped the sound of Rafe's laughter with his friend, to come here. She'd lost track of how long she'd been standing, looking out and trying not to think, when the heavy door opened behind her. She turned as the man she'd been trying not to think about stepped into the room. He paused, clearly not expecting to see her here. "Is the party over?" she asked.

"Still going." He gave a half smile. "I bailed. Thought I'd come up here for a little time-out."

Lexie took a single step away from the window. "You stay," she said. "I was just going."

But as he crossed to her she didn't seem able to move any farther.

"It's so beautiful up here," she said.

"Yes," he said, his gaze never leaving her face. He stopped in front of her and brushed a thumb across her cheek. Did that mean he'd seen the telltale tracks of her tears?

"I'm leaving." She didn't know whether she spoke the words for his benefit or for hers. The only thing she did know was that the prospect of her departure was a dark, yawning chasm. The thought of leaving San Philippe forever. The thought of leaving Rafe. Forever. It weighed almost unbearably on her.

"I know." He lowered his head and placed the gentlest of kisses on each of her cheekbones. And then he pulled her into his arms and she went willingly. He held her tightly to him and she absorbed the sensation of being pressed against him, tried to commit it to memory, tried to detail each part of her that touched him and where and how, the feel of his cheek resting on her head, his arms around her.

She tilted her head up to look at him, to study his face. He returned her scrutiny for the longest time. And then he kissed her. Soft and gentle, the knowledge of her leaving in his kiss. She tasted the faint trace of champagne on his lips.

What started out soft and gentle grew heated and hungry. Breathing hard, Rafe lifted his head. "We shouldn't. *I* shouldn't."

She pulled his head back down. "We should." She smiled against his lips, heedless. "I'm leaving anyway. What can it hurt now?"

"It can hurt you. You deserve better. Someone needs to look out for you, and if you won't protect yourself from me then I have to do it."

"I deserve this. After all you've put me through, I deserve *this*."

But still he backed away.

Lexie pulled the silk ribbon that held the front of her dress in place and the dress fell open. "Don't go."

"That's a low trick, Lex." Rafe stopped dead. "It wouldn't be humanly possible now." He walked slowly back to her. "Have I told you red is my favorite color?" He looked into her eyes as he pushed her dress from her shoulders, smiled as it pooled at her feet, then trailed his fingers in its wake to touch the red of her bra, and then her panties. "Do you know what you do to me?"

"I'm hoping it's something like what you do to me."

As he slid his hands to her waist, and slowly up and round, she trembled beneath his touch. His fingers found the clasp they sought, and her bra whispered to the floor.

She gasped as he knelt before her and pressed a kiss

to the center of her panties. And then he drew the fine lace from her hips, over her thighs.

One more kiss, and another gasp. He trailed more kisses upward, another to her belly, between her breasts, her neck. With her eyes on him he undid his buttons. He discarded his shirt, his pants, his boxers. No pretence, no barriers. Till he stood before her, bathed in golden sunlight, strong and proud and hers.

For now.

Him. Her. Nothing else.

He reached for her hair, ran his fingers through its sun-warmed length, ran his hands over the curve of her shoulders, down her arms till his hands founds hers.

Holding her gaze, he lifted her hands and pressed a kiss to the back of each. Then, lowering his hands, he slid his fingers between hers, stretching them apart. Palms touched, breath mingled.

And then he touched his lips to hers, with a gentleness born of constraint.

She moved. Closed the gap between them till her breasts pressed against his chest and her belly pressed against his erection.

He pulled her closer still, hard against him, deepening the kiss at the same time, and they moved together, legs twining, hands searching, all the while each drinking in the taste of the other.

Kissing, they made it as far as the center of the room and then no farther. Dropping to their knees on the rug, hands and lips had free rein.

Lexie pushed him back and he pulled her with him.

She straddled him and then sheathed herself on him, loving the feel of him in her, under her. Loving him.

He was hers.

For now.

He lifted his hands to her breasts, caressed and kneaded. He pulled her forward so he could take a nipple in his mouth. His hands shifted to her waist, her hips, and he was pushing into her deeper, pulling her onto him harder.

She rode his thrusts, and he drove her higher, further, into darkness and light. And then she was gasping, whimpering. Her eyes flew open, locked on his, all beauty and blind passion, and together they cried out.

Lexie fell forward onto him, her hair curtaining his face, her body pulsing around his.

And he held her tight to him.

In the darkness, Lexie clung to Rafe's hand, keeping close as he led her through the castle's dimly lit halls. They'd made love again and again in the turret room. And then slept. And now, in the small hours, they found their way, stumbling and laughing, through corridors and downstairs.

He stopped outside a door, pushed it open and led her into a room. Lit only by the light of the moon, Lexie could still see it was a bedroom. *Rafe's* bedroom.

Not releasing her hand, he crossed with her to the massive sleigh bed. He lifted his hands to her hair. "We should sleep."

"Yes." They should. She had no idea what time it was, knew only that it was late or very early. But she slipped her hands around his waist, pressed her lips to his. She had this one stolen night with him. She wouldn't waste it. She pulled him unresisting down with her onto the bed, reveled in the weight of him on her and over her.

And after the rug and the couch of the turret room, his broad bed was a novelty. Room to roll and tangle and laugh and touch.

Lexie woke with sunlight warming one side of her face and Rafe's chest warming the other side. His heart beat strong and steady beneath her cheek. His arms rested loosely around her. As she woke fully, she basked in the magic, the beauty, of being with him.

She tilted her face up to see him watching her and then pulled away to see him better.

He let her go, his hands trailing from her.

Instantly, she regretted pulling away. When she'd been lying close, touching, eyes closed, anything had been possible. There had at least been a fragile hope of a glittering future. That they—she and Rafe—might be possible.

Now, lying on her side, she studied him. Rumpled hair, beard-shadowed jaw and a slow, sexy smile, but it was the wariness in his dark eyes that pierced the fragile magic of the morning, that sucked away her happiness.

And she knew in that moment that she should never have come to his room, should never have fallen asleep with him so that they then had to navigate waking up together. The memories of their night together would now forever end with this.

She'd given up her dreams because of him. But not *for* him. She knew not to allow herself to be that stupid. But she hadn't been able to love his brother when her every thought had been of Rafe. When she had felt things for Rafe and wanted things from Rafe that she would never feel or want from Adam.

She was leaving today. And she knew he wouldn't, couldn't, offer her a future. And yet here she lay, wanting precisely that. A future. With Rafe.

Not the man of her dreams, but the man of her realities. The man who understood her and made her laugh and made her want him.

The wariness in his eyes now froze her hopes, her heart. She could almost see the regrets and his questions and fears. Would she want to marry him now, want to have his babies, want to trap him? Already he was formulating words to soften his rejection.

She had wanted, desperately, to make love with him, but not to love him, to fall in love with him. She hadn't wanted that. But heaven help her, looking at him now, feeling already the pain in her heart, she realized that she had fallen anyway. So the answer to those fearful questions in his eyes was—yes, she wanted to marry him and yes, she wanted to have his babies. And most of all she wanted him to love her. But no, she didn't want to trap him.

"Lexie." His voice had the sexiest early-morning rasp.

She touched a finger to his lips. "I don't think you should say anything. I don't want regrets or excuses, and I couldn't bear false promises. I'm here, in your bed, and I know that's breaking all your rules, but it wasn't planned.

"I'm going today, we both knew that, so we both knew last night was just…last night. And this morning is this morning. So don't say anything. Unless of course it's 'make love with me right now.'" She tried to make it a joke. But even though there was only a hollow space where her heart used to be, the rest of her still wanted him. Just once more. And that need had slipped through in her voice.

She saw his hesitation even as he lifted his hand to touch her hair. The warm lips parted beneath her fingertip, but no words came out.

She slipped from the bed.

He made no move to stop her.

At the door to the bathroom she turned back and tried to smile. Giving up, she swallowed past the lump in her throat. "Last night was perfect. Thank you."

Eleven

Rafe stood on the lowest of the palace steps. Cloaked in the royal Marconi calm that revealed nothing of their private thoughts, his father, brother and sister were gathered around Lexie. She hugged each of them in turn, then looked for him. He stepped down. Neither royal protocol nor experience had prepared him to bid farewell to a woman like Lexie. A woman who meant the things Lexie meant to him.

Mere hours ago she had been in his bed. It had killed him, not asking—begging—her to stay, in his bed, in his life. But he'd shattered enough of her dreams. She deserved her fairy tale. Despite his title, he was no one's fairy tale, and never would be.

Dry-eyed, she walked to him. Pale and strong and… the most beautiful woman he'd ever known. A soul-deep beauty, rare and precious. He couldn't stop himself, he touched a hand to her hair, her jaw, tried to commit to memory the feel of her, even though forgetting her was critical to his future happiness. He hadn't been going to embrace her, but she stepped into his arms, and if his life had depended on it, he couldn't have avoided wrapping them around her for the chance of holding her to him one last time.

She was the one to break the contact, stepping away from him. For a moment he saw the question and hope in her eyes. The same look he'd seen when she woke up in his arms this morning.

Then she smiled, and it was the saddest smile he'd ever seen. Clenching his fists, he kept his hands at his sides. "I didn't mean to make you sad, Lex," he said quietly. "If I could take back last night, for your sake, I would. We should have ended with the day before yesterday. That was what I wanted to give you."

If anything, her smile grew both sadder and brighter. "I wouldn't," she answered. "That day was perfect. But last night was even better."

"You'll find a good man. One worthy of you. One who's everything he should be. Better than Adam. Better than me." Someone who loved her for who she was. Someone who could offer her marriage and the family she wanted. Someone who'd treat her with respect and reverence. Not someone who couldn't even wait till they got to the other side of a room but dragged her down to a rug on the floor.

"My only requirement is that he loves me."

"He'd be a fool not to."

"There's no shortage of fools."

She got into the waiting car and he watched it pull away, seeming to pull a piece of him with it.

Lexie's departure was vastly different from her arrival. No eager, waving crowds waited at the airport. A fact for which she was deeply grateful. A handful of photographers loitered at the barriers, doubtless waiting to document the fact that the woman who'd spurned their favorite prince and been spurned in turn by the other one did actually leave their country.

Joseph, the head of security, escorted her across the tarmac and up the stairs to the jet. She knew it was meant as a courtesy. It felt like she was being seen off the premises, that like the press, he wanted to make sure she really did go, that there would be an end to the havoc she'd wrought.

She wanted that end, too, to the havoc of her personal and emotional life, though she knew the pain was only just beginning.

On board she sank onto one of the deep cream couches and did up her seatbelt at the gentle prompting of the hostess. Lexie had deliberately chosen the couch because it didn't face a window. She closed her eyes and waited. Finally the tone of the jet's engines changed and they began to taxi along the runway. She resisted the urge to take one last look at San Philippe as they gathered speed and then became airborne. The wheels locked back up into the undercarriage with a thudding finality.

She'd expected tears, but they never came. All she felt was a great, welling hollowness.

So much for not making a spectacle of herself. She'd done that and so much worse.

She heard a sound in the cabin. The hostess. If only she could be left alone. "I'm fine, thanks," she said. "I don't need anything."

"Or anyone?" a deep, achingly familiar voice asked.

Her eyes flew open and she drank in the sight of Rafe as he smiled down at her and then lowered himself onto the couch beside her. "What are you doing here?" She was almost afraid to ask. "How did you even get here?"

He took her hand, held tight to it. "The second question's easy to answer. I took a leaf out of your book and came by motorbike. I passed you just before the airport."

"And the first question?" She clung to his hand like a lifeline. So much depended on his answer. Hope filled her, but she'd had her hopes dashed before now and the prospect of it happening again terrified her.

"A, I'm not a fool and B, I'm not a martyr."

That was no answer. At least not one she understood. "Meaning?"

"I said only a fool wouldn't love you. And clearly I'm not a fool because I do—love you. I don't know when or how it happened. I wanted you almost from the start, from the time I first saw you in the nightclub, no surprise there. I'd wanted women before, so I didn't think it was anything I couldn't control." He made a derisive sound.

A laugh cut short. "But the wanting that started that night has only grown stronger, become something more than I even believed existed—love." He shrugged, but the grip on her hand tightened. "And the love is well out of my control. I've got no idea how it even happened and only one idea of what to do about it." He ran gentle fingers down a lock of her hair, reverently touched her face.

The hostess appeared, took one look at them and just as quickly disappeared.

"I didn't mean it to happen, Lex, but it did. And till half an hour ago I thought letting you go was the right thing to do, which is when I remembered I'm not a martyr. I'm not willing to sacrifice my happiness while you look for someone worthy of you. I want to be the one you wake up with every morning. Though I know I'm not your fairy tale."

She opened her mouth to argue, but he silenced her with a finger to her lips. "Let me finish, Lex. This isn't easy for me, but I need to say it, need you to hear it." When she nodded, he continued. "I know I'm not the one you wanted to love. And I know there are better men out there than me. But I can't let them have you. At least not without offering myself to you first. I want to marry you, to be yours, to make you mine. I want all the things I never thought I would. Knowing you has changed so much for me, for the better. But it was only the awful prospect of actually losing you that forced me to see it."

He searched her face and then in a sudden movement swooped in, covered her lips with his and kissed her.

And she clung to him, kissed him back, drank in the taste of him, reveled in the feel of him. She didn't have the willpower or even the desire to deny him.

Too soon, he broke the kiss, rested his forehead against hers. His hands cupped her jaw, his fingers threading into her hair. She held him, breathed in his scent, drew it deep within her, resented having to exhale and lose that part of him she'd captured. Her weakness for him was absolute.

He took her hands again, folding strong, sure fingers around hers. "Say you'll have me?"

She was desperate to say yes and yet she couldn't. "Rafe—" she clung to his hands, the contact imperative "—you haven't thought this through. You once said you were trying to protect me from you. But it's you who needs to be protected from me. Think about your father and your country. Think about what the press will say."

"I don't care what anyone other than you says. And, in case you haven't noticed, I'm still waiting for a yes here."

"I care what they say about you. They'll vilify you."

"Not just me." He smiled. "You, too. But not for long. And at least we'll be in it together. I'll get us through it. Trust me, I've had practice. Besides, you haven't seen this morning's papers, have you?"

"No. I couldn't bear it anymore."

"It's not all bad news. Some bright spark in the press corps has realized that my father only ever said he had given permission for his son and Alexia Wyndham Jones to marry. He never said which son. So along with all the photos of you and me together, the press are speculating that this is what Dad, the master manipulator, meant all along, that he was playing them. They're rewriting history to suit themselves. And Dad'll be happy to go along with it."

"He couldn't possibly have had any idea that we'd fall in love."

"So you do love me?" He studied her face.

She paused, unable to deny this man a moment longer. "With all my heart."

"And do you mind if we don't do the big royal wedding thing?"

"I don't mind at all." She was still trying to process what was happening. That Rafe loved her, that he wanted to wake up with her every morning.

"Good." He smiled. "Because my father's not the only wily one. I have it all figured out. The pilot's already changed the flight plan. We're heading to Vegas. And we're getting married. Today. May as well give the press something to get really worked up about. We can be San Philippe's Rebel Royals. And in tricking them and denying them all their royal wedding, we'll have sunk so low that the only way to go will be upward in the public's opinion. And as soon as you have my babies everyone, but me especially, will be happy. All will be forgiven and forgotten."

He lifted her hand, covering it with his other so that it disappeared within his clasp. "Lex, you're a part of me that I hadn't even realized was missing. The best part." Tenderness shone in his dark eyes. He released her hand to cup her face, and she pressed her cheek against the warmth of his palm. "Alexia Wyndham Jones, Lexie, my Lexie. I love you. You are my Everest, my everything."

Finally, finally he kissed her again and she knew despite what he'd said, she had her fairy tale.

* * * * *

COMING NEXT MONTH

Available July 13, 2010

#2023 THE MILLIONAIRE MEETS HIS MATCH
Kate Carlisle
Man of the Month

**#2024 CLAIMING HER BILLION-DOLLAR
BIRTHRIGHT**
Maureen Child
Dynasties: The Jarrods

#2025 IN TOO DEEP
"Husband Material"—Brenda Jackson
"The Sheikh's Bargained Bride"—Olivia Gates
A Summer for Scandal

#2026 VIRGIN PRINCESS, TYCOON'S TEMPTATION
Michelle Celmer
Royal Seductions

#2027 SEDUCTION ON THE CEO'S TERMS
Charlene Sands
Napa Valley Vows

**#2028 THE SECRETARY'S
BOSSMAN BARGAIN**
Red Garnier

SDCNM0610

REQUEST YOUR FREE BOOKS!

2 FREE NOVELS PLUS 2 FREE GIFTS!

 Silhouette® Desire®

Passionate, Powerful, Provocative!

SDES10R

HARLEQUIN®

A *Romance*

FOR EVERY MOOD™

Spotlight on
— Heart & Home —

Heartwarming romances
where love can happen
right when you least expect it.

See the next page to enjoy a sneak peek
from Silhouette Special Edition®,
a Heart and Home series.

*Introducing McFARLANE'S PERFECT BRIDE
by USA TODAY bestselling author Christine Rimmer,
from Silhouette Special Edition®.*

Entranced. Captivated. Enchanted.

Connor sat across the table from Tori Jones and
couldn't help thinking that those words exactly described
what effect the small-town schoolteacher had on him.
He might as well stop trying to tell himself he wasn't
interested. He was powerfully drawn to her.

Clearly, he should have dated more when he was
younger.

There had been a couple of other women since Jennifer
had walked out on him. But he had never been entranced.
Or captivated. Or enchanted.

Until now.

He wanted her—*her,* Tori Jones, in particular. Not just
someone suitably attractive and well-bred, as Jennifer had
been. Not just someone sophisticated, sexually exciting
and discreet, which pretty much described the two women
he'd dated after his marriage crashed and burned.

It came to him that he...he *liked* this woman. And that
was new to him. He liked her quick wit, her wisdom and
her big heart. He liked the passion in her voice when she
talked about things she believed in.

He liked *her.* And suddenly it mattered all out of
proportion that she might like him, too.

Was he losing it? He couldn't help but wonder. Was
he cracking under the strain—of the soured economy, the
McFarlane House setbacks, his divorce, the scary changes
in his son? Of the changes he'd decided he needed to make
in his life and himself?

Strangely, right then, on his first date with Tori Jones, he didn't care if he just might be going over the edge. He was having a great time—having *fun,* of all things—and he didn't want it to end.

Is Connor finally able to admit his feelings to Tori, and are they reciprocated?
Find out in McFARLANE'S PERFECT BRIDE
by USA TODAY *bestselling author Christine Rimmer.*
Available July 2010,
only from Silhouette Special Edition®.